Jerry Pournelle

BIRTH OF FIRE

PUBLISHED BY POCKET BOOKS NEW YORK

POCKET BOOKS, a Simon & Schuster division of
GULF & WESTERN CORPORATION
1230 Avenue of the Americas, New York, N.Y. 10020

ISBN: 0-671-41614-6

First Pocket Books printing August, 1978

10   9   8   7   6   5   4   3   2

POCKET and colophon are trademarks of Simon & Schuster.

Printed in the U.S.A.

FOR
SARGE WORKMAN

BIRTH
OF FIRE

1

"Here they come!" Our war leader crawled up to where I was crouched behind a garbage can. "You ready, Garrett?"

"As I'll ever be." I don't mind saying I was scared. We'd been in plenty of stomps before, but this one looked to be bad. The word was out that the Hackers had guns.

I patted my clothes to check weapons. As well as the bowie knife in my hand, I had four throwing knives, each in its hand-sewn pocket on the left side of my jacket, a chain in my regular jacket pocket, and a two-foot section of iron pipe in my belt. "I'm ready," I said.

"Good. We're counting on you." Spinny crawled off to encourage the other troops.

I was scared all right, but I felt pretty good, too. I was the hidden reserve, waiting in ambush to break some heads and show just how much better we were than those goons could ever be. I had tough comrades around me, and they depended on me. At the back of my mind I may have wished I was somewhere else, but you don't let thoughts like that up front when you're going into a fight. When this was over we'd own this part of Baltimore.

We were in a big open space under the Washington slideway. When they built the rolling roads, they left a lot of the old streets down under. There were shops and stores but not many customers wanted to go down there, so Undertown belonged to gangs and clubs. Like ours. Our official name was Werewolves, but we called ourselves Dog Soldiers, and we were a proud lot. I was vice-president.

The first Hackers moved into the square and some of ours hit them from the sides. More Hackers moved in; I waited. When I had their guns spotted, I'd come in from behind.

Spinny had planned it that way, but it didn't go. Just as a free-for-all developed in the square, three Hackers came out of a window we'd been sure was boarded up tight. They'd loosened the nails earlier in the day. Now they jumped me from behind.

I turned and flicked a knife at the nearest one. It hit him in the arm and he dropped back. That gave me time to get my chain out and the other two backed off a step, but not for long. They had obviously worked together before. As I bent to avoid a karate-style kick from one of them, the other laid a ball bat alongside my head. It staggered me despite the surplus Federation Army helmet I wore.

Some plan, I thought. Crap. Ambush my ass! I was bigger than most of the other Dogs, and although at 20 I wasn't the oldest member, I was either the best or second-best fighter we had. I was supposed to be out there picking off Hackers from behind. Instead, I was alone and cornered. It looked like I'd end up with kicked-in ribs and a skull fracture if I was lucky—and my luck hadn't been running any too good.

I caught the guy who had the ball bat with the end of my chain. It whipped around one knee and he fell. I aimed a kick at his head, but missed. Then the other one was on me.

The last thing I remember was a gun going off, three times, and those damned sirens.

* * *

I woke up in jail. I wasn't bad hurt, but I was in big trouble. The cops had got there just as I went down, and two cops were killed in the fight. They'd been shot, and we hadn't had any guns, so it must have been the Hackers, but even if they believed us that cut no ice with the cops. They were out to make examples of us.

The problem was the cops didn't have anybody to stick it to. They had several dead bodies besides their own two, but the live crop consisted of seven juveniles—and me. The juvenile court wasn't about to let the cops take it out on those poor children.

The cops offered me a couple of deals if I'd name some others and go state's evidence, but aside from the fact that it would be suicide, I'm no fink. Since they had only one adult to make an example of, it didn't look too good for Garrett Pittson.

I can't help my name. Garrett means "brave spear." I didn't have to look it up; my father told me. That gives you some idea of where my old man's head was when I was born. He'd just retired after twenty years in the old U.S. Army, back before the Federation abolished national forces. Though he'd been in communications and couldn't have seen much fighting, he talked like he'd won all the brushfires that the U.S. had ever been in, single-handedly beating the enemy to death with his walkie-talkie.

He and my mother had great ambitions for me. I had a normal childhood, with maybe more bloodthirsty tales told me than most kids get, but nothing special. I went through a public high school where I was taught to read and write, which is more than a lot can say they learned, and got interested in electronics because my old man had the junk lying around the place, and it was fun to tinker with. It wasn't their fault things didn't turn out right.

When I got out of high school, things went to hell. I wasn't quite bright enough for a scholarship to a good college. Oh, I had decent enough grades in subjects I was interested in, but there weren't that many interesting subjects. And I liked to read, but not the books on the approved list.

Worse yet, we didn't belong to any minority groups, and we weren't quite poor enough for nondiscriminatory government aid. We sure weren't rich enough for me to go to a good college without assistance. That left the local community junior college, with plans for transfer to the state university after two years.

It didn't work. The instructors had nothing to say and weren't interested in teaching anyway. To them, it was just another job. They never talked about anything that wasn't in the stupid books they gave us, and there wasn't much in those. I could read the books and not bother with the classes. I decided I didn't want to be an engineer after all.

I didn't know what I wanted to be. The best jobs were with the government, of course. Get on civil service and stay there. It wasn't what I wanted to do with my life; I wanted to get out on my own, do something for myself. But how?

The government didn't let you do that. The government took care of you, whether you wanted to be taken care of or not. Even the dropout communes were visited by the government social workers. But if they didn't let you starve, they didn't let you get ahead, either. That's called social justice.

I wasn't interested in my classes and I wasn't interested in where I was going, and so I took to hanging around with other kids my age. At least we could earn some respect from each other; as part of proving our manhood we did some things that weren't strictly legal. Pretty soon we were in trouble with the police.

It wasn't serious, but three times my father had to come to the station house and get me out. The third time I was home just long enough to pack. My old man threw me out of the house for a lazy bum.

Hell, I *was* a lazy bum. He hadn't made any mistake there. I had no ambition, and while I didn't mind working —I could and did put in twenty-hour days on hobby stuff when I felt like it—I didn't see anything to work *for*. I wasn't going to be a rich taxpayer without graduating from something better than Francis Scott Key Community College. Any job I'd get with a degree from that joint would earn me just a little more than welfare and be about as interesting as carrying out the kitty box.

When my old man threw me out we had a hell of a fight, and right then I decided that I was on my own. I needed no help from him. But I had no job; pretty soon I drifted down to Undertown. You can't stay alive down there unless you're part of a gang. I chose the Dog Soldiers, and before long I was proud to be part of it. Sure, I knew there was no future in it. So what? There was no future in anything else I could find, and this was a good gang.

Up to the big fight that was the story of my life. It wasn't much of a story. I thought about that a lot while I sat in the cells waiting for trial. Here I was, twenty years old, and not worth a damn to myself or anybody else.

Well, I told myself, that doesn't matter much. It looks like I've got a great future stamping out license plates, with occasional groovy variety like laundry duty and sewing mailbags.

* * *

The judge didn't like me. He was up for reelection, and the newspapers were giving him hell for turning criminals loose. The cops were pushing hard to have the book thrown at me, and the Public Defender didn't think my case was going to give him the headlines he'd need to set up a rich private practice.

They charged me with murder one, and it took the jury about ten minutes to come in and say "guilty." I read somewhere that English judges used to put on a black cap before they gave out death sentences. We didn't have death sentences and he didn't have a black cap, but if we did and he did, he would have. He socked me twenty years to life. Then they herded me back into the cells.

My deputy public defender could spare me a half hour. He laid it out for me in simple terms.

"Go to prison and you'll be a faggot inside of three years. You've seen the queens in your cell block?"

"Not me." I had nothing against homos, but I had no desire to join them.

"Yeah. Well, if you hold out, you still won't like it. Be a good boy. Work hard and they may let you out in ten years if you crawl just right. How are you at arse-kissing? Can you suck up to the parole board?"

"I'd be more likely to tell 'em to rape themselves." I never was much at the arse-kissing game. I guess I learned more from my old man than I like to admit.

"Well, there you are," he said.

He looked so goddamn smug. He wasn't on my side of the damned wire fence. "What the hell do you mean, there I am? Why are you talking to me?"

"Don't get smart with me, Pittson. I came to offer you a choice."

13

"What choice have I got?"

"I can put in for a new trial. Maybe I can get one. You could get out on bail. Can you raise a hundred grand?"

"That's stupid."

"Yeah. And even if a bondsman would handle you, which I doubt, you haven't got the ten grand he'll want. So you stay inside for the new trial. And there's not a chance in hell that the verdict will be any different next time."

"Okay. So a new trial is a waste of time." So was this conversation, but it was better in the visiting room than in the cell.

"Yes. You can't stay out of prison—if you stay here. But you've got another option: voluntary exile, transportation for life. I can arrange it for you."

I didn't have to think about it, not really. I already knew my answer. I'd read about the colony program and how they needed more men. There'd been a time or two, back at Francis Scott Key, when I toyed with the idea of shipping out as a volunteer.

It sure as hell beat what I had coming here. Why not go to Mars?

"Where do I sign up?"

2

Mars is a bleak place, but it was exciting to be there just
the same. They trooped us into a clear plastic dome where
we got our first look at the outside. It was a big dome, a
couple of hundred feet across, and not at all safe, but they
didn't tell us that.

The thing that struck me most was the stars. It was
daylight outside, and although the sun looked a little
small, it seemed about as bright as I remembered it being on Earth. The next thing I noticed was the sharp out-
line of the shadows: Mars boasted the darkest shadows
I'd ever seen—although everything the sun hit was
brightly lit. That was strange enough, but the stars got to
me.

The sky was pink at the horizon, real pink, and you
couldn't see stars there, but straight overhead they were
glorious. There were more than I'd ever seen in Baltimore's smoggy nighttime skies. My old man had taken
me out in the country once. We had to drive damn near
a thousand miles, and he never did it again, but we looked
at stars, and they were beautiful. Now I was looking at
stars in daytime.

The camp was located at the edge of a rugged, dust-
covered plain. I found out later that Hellas Basin

stretched out fifteen hundred miles to the southeast, so it wasn't surprising that I couldn't see across it. Boulders were piled every which way out there, bright on the sunny side, dark as night in the shade. Anything might hide in those shadows. Once I thought I saw something moving.

North and curving east rugged mountains stuck straight up into the dark sky. Some had pointed tops, but a lot more were jagged-rimmed craters, while some had flat tops like Arizona mesas. The tallest had wispy clouds stringing out from their peaks.

Two big tractors covered with little bright-blue squares were crawling out of the mountains toward us. Their treads threw up clouds of dust that fell in slow motion back onto the plain.

I don't remember much about the trip out. They shipped us in cold sleep, stacked in tubes like expensive cigars. About one in ten never woke up. That's one reason people don't volunteer to be colonists.

I hadn't been enthusiastic about the cold sleep myself, but it seemed like better odds than what I was facing if I stayed on Earth.

I looked at my fellow transportees, wondering what had made them choose to come here. Reasons much like my own, I decided. We were a pretty scruffy lot.

We stank. We didn't walk any too good, either, because we weren't used to the 40 percent gravity. Low gravity's tricky. It makes you feel light—hell, you *are* light—but you've still got the same mass. If you turn a corner fast, your legs go out from under you. Walking takes a peculiar gait, and running takes a lot of practice.

Actually, we didn't reek anywhere near as much as we should have. Not that we were clean. The air was thin. They kept the pressure lower than on Earth, about ten pounds rather than Earth's nearly fifteen. You had to shout to be heard very far away, and nothing smelled right. Food didn't taste too good—but for the moment, in that company, with no bath water for weeks and none likely, the thin air seemed a blessing.

Of course I didn't know a single person there. There'd been too little time since we were taken out of our cigar cans and put on our feet—those of us who woke up. We were dressed in welfare coveralls. We were all ages, but most were older than me. Out of the hundred of us, only six were women. The youngest one was thirty and she looked older.

The women tended to cluster. A herd of men circled around them; I didn't see any point in joining that game. Not yet. I could wait to see what choices I had. If any.

We were all white North Americans. The Federation goes through phases in its policies, and just then there was a lot of pressure not to ship blacks to Mars because it was cruel and unusual punishment. There's some chance of getting home from the Moon, but Mars is strictly a one-way trip.

I thought about that, and shrugged to myself. Okay, I'm here, I thought. So I'll make the best of it. The landscape was more interesting than my fellow convicts, so I turned back to it.

The tractors were closer now. They were big boxy things, with wings sticking out from the sides so they could carry more of the blue solar-power cells. The cells took in sunlight and gave out electricity. I knew about them; I was more fascinated with the slow-motion fall of the dust.

There wasn't much wind out there at the time, but I'd heard the Federation guards say that sometimes there were dust hurricanes, with winds of more than three-hundred miles an hour. That, I thought, would be something to see. A man out there would be blown away like toilet paper in front of a fan. For a moment I wanted nothing to do with this planet.

I'd better learn, though, I told myself. This is home. Feel the low gravity. Talking about low gravs in school didn't mean anything, but now I'm in it. I'd heard people can live to be two hundred on Mars because of that low gravity, only they don't because Mars kills them first. There are a lot of ways to die here. So learn or die.

"HEAR THIS ALL PILGRIMS. NEW ARRIVALS REPORT TO THE MAIN HALL. ON THE DOUBLE." The speaker said that three times, then repeated it in Spanish.

The guards started moving through the crowd to hurry us along. They were all a little older than me, all convicts who'd been recruited into Federation Service, with a few Federation troopers from the volunteer army. They didn't like Pilgrims. They were slaves, too, but slaves with weapons and power—the worst kind of slavemasters.

"On the double," one said. He laid his billy club against my butt. It splatted, and it hurt. I balled a fist and turned toward him. He was grinning. "Want to try it?" he asked.

"No." I turned away and headed for the main hall. No point in getting my skull bashed in for nothing, but it rankled that I had to take that.

"Always they push you around," someone said behind me. I turned to see a white-haired old man. "Always they tell you what to do. It is the arrogance of power. They think of nothing but to hurt people, to beat them, to show how important they are. Some day we will take that power away from them."

"Yeah, sure," I said. In about a million years. I could walk faster than him, and I did.

He tried to keep up. "I am Aristotle O'Brien," he said. "You may laugh at the name if you like."

I didn't want to laugh at his name, I wanted to get the hell away from him before he got me in trouble. I didn't figure I owed him anything. As far as I was concerned the first rule was to keep my mouth shut and stay out of trouble until I knew what the score was. That lonely old man could have been my grandfather, but he hadn't learned that first rule, and probably he never would.

I put on the speed and left him. I wasn't too proud of that, leaving a lonely old man with no friends, no one to talk to, no one to help him feel human. I wasn't very proud, but I left him.

The main assembly hall, like all of Hellastown except for the dome, was underground. The walls of the tunnel leading down to it were concrete, but of a funny color—red, like the dust outside. The air stank from too many people with too little wash water. The ramp down was steep and hard to walk on. Just ahead of me was a giant, the biggest man of our group, one of the biggest men I'd ever seen. Kelso, his name was, and he was a good bit taller than my six feet. On Earth he would have weighed over two hundred and fifty pounds, no fat.

The assembly hall could have held ten times the hundred of us. It had seats and a stage. The stage was crowded with junk, such as a portable field organ like military chaplains use, a big plaster relief map, a blackboard, and a movie projection screen. Overhead were a bunch of faded streamers, old decorations of some kind.

There wasn't any wood in the room. I thought about that for a second and realized I hadn't seen any wood since I got to Mars. Even the guards' billy clubs were plastic.

The furniture was stone, concrete, iron, or plastic, none of it painted. A panel of colored glass was set high up above the stage, some kind of Mars landscape with human figures in the foreground. They were all out on the surface without suits and there was a bright blue sky all around, overhead as well as at the horizon. Idly, I wondered what it meant.

Most of the men crowded around the women. They kept pushing and shoving to get near them. Kelso plowed his way through the press until he was next to a big-chested woman with flaring hips and tight coveralls. She grinned at him. "You're a big one, aren't you, ducks?"

He started to answer, but someone shoved him. "Who the hell you pushing?" he yelled. The other guy answered, which was a mistake. Kelso reached out and picked him up. He held him off the ground for a moment, then tossed him. The guy sailed ten feet. Low gravity, but it was impressive anyway.

That's when the riot started. The guy had friends, and a half dozen of them set on Kelso.

"Break it up." The guard sounded bored. When nobody paid any attention he waded into the fight. He raised his billy club and brought it down on one head, then another. He didn't care who he hit, and I was damned glad I wasn't anywhere near that fight.

Kelso got whacked with the billy club and grabbed for the guard. But by then some other guards had come rushing over, and more came through a door into the hall. Pretty soon they had Kelso wrapped up and were beating on his head. Every now and then Kelso would get an arm free and send one flying. Everybody else stood back to watch. Kelso against the guards.

It was stupid. He couldn't win. But goddamn, what a man! I wished I had the nerve to do what he was doing. It might be worth the lumps to have somebody to strike out at.

The fight didn't last long, though, and when it was over

Kelso was bleeding from a dozen places, his hands were cuffed and he was sprawled out across a bench, not quite out cold.

"Was it worth it?"

A man had come onto the stage while we were watching the fight. He was about fifty, dressed in gray green coveralls with three black bands at the ends of the sleeves. He wore what seemed to be a skintight body stocking under the coveralls. "I asked, 'Was it worth it?'" he demanded. "Anyone here think it was?"

There was a lot of talk, mostly babble. One of the guards picked up Kelso's shoulders. Another grabbed his feet.

"Leave him there," the man on the stage ordered. The guards shrugged and dropped Kelso. His head banged on the bench. I could hear it all the way over where I was. One of the guards laughed.

"And the rest of you, shut up!" the man said. His voice had that quality in it: you knew he was used to being obeyed. It cut right through the babble. We were quiet.

"My name is Alexander Farr, and I am superintendent here. You might like it better if I said warden." Farr talked without using a microphone. We could hear him fine.

"You'll get more lectures, this talk's unofficial. You can go to sleep if you like. I don't advise it."

Farr reminded me of a science teacher I'd once had. The teacher used to say we could go to sleep, but he'd been willing to help you learn, as long as you wanted him to. He'd gone out of his way to teach things that weren't part of the usual program at the school. Because he didn't try to force it down my throat I'd got interested, and I learned more science than I'd thought I would.

The superintendent wasn't a very big man. He sat on the edge of the stage and his legs didn't reach the floor. He dangled them and kicked them back and forth. "Smoke 'em if you got 'em," he said. "If you're smart, you won't. Tobacco's too bloody expensive out here. Save two ways by quitting. You don't have to buy 'em, and you can sell what you've got to some sucker who's hooked."

That was no problem for me. The Dog Soldiers didn't use pot, and I'd never got interested in tobacco. One of the men handed a cigarette to the middle-aged woman in the row in front of him. He lit hers, then lit one for himself and blew a smoke ring right at the stage.

If Farr noticed he didn't show it. "You'll get the official garbage later," he said. "What I'm giving you now is the straight skinny. Hear and believe." He looked down at Kelso. "How you doing?"

Kelso grunted and tried to sit up.

"Going to behave now? Or do you like being cuffed?"

"I'm okay," Kelso said.

"Didn't ask that." Farr's tone showed curiosity but not much concern.

"I'll be a good boy."

Farr nodded. "Right. Corporal, take those cuffs off him."

"Yes, sir." The guard unlocked the handcuffs. He didn't bother to lower his voice as he told Kelso, "Next time I'll break your goddamn skull for you."

"Hear and believe," Farr said. "Okay, chums, let me give you the facts of life. Number one. Don't try to escape. There's no place to go. If you make it outside, you'll live about fifteen seconds. There's no air out there, and your blood will boil away in your veins. It's not a pretty way to go, and I'm told it's painful as hell.

"Number two. Don't try to escape. You may think you're smart and see a way to get a p-suit. You may even be able to operate it. And then what? You can't make air, and you can't carry enough to get anywhere worth going. Running out of air's not a lot better than going out without a suit.

"Number three. Don't try to escape. Sure there's a town here, and sure there are a lot of people in it. But you'll pay for everything, and I do mean everything."

He lifted an orange disk that hung from a chain around his neck. I'd noticed that everyone except us newcomers wore one, but they weren't all the same color. "Air-tax receipt," Farr said. "Mine's orange because I'm due to have it recharged. If it turns red, that's it. Pay up or go outside. You'll need air medals, because God help you if anybody catches you in town without one."

"Why? What happens?" someone demanded.

"Outside," Farr said. "Not even a chance to pay up. Just out."

"And who's to put me out?" Kelso demanded.

Farr grinned. "Every man jack who's paid his taxes, that's who. Might take several for you, but they'll do it."

"This is not fair." I recognized the voice. Old Aristotle O'Brien. "Not fair," he repeated.

"Probably not," Farr said. "But it's the way things are." He grinned. His teeth had two gaps, and they gave him a ferocious look.

"Number four," Farr said. "Don't try to escape. We're going to give you a crash course in survival. Pay attention and you might stay alive. While you're taking the course, there won't be any Mickey Mouse crap. You'll get food to eat, water to drink, and air to breathe. The only work you have is the classes and some general crud like keeping the barracks clean and helping out in the kitchen. I guarantee you won't find anyplace you could escape to as pleasant as where you are now."

"What happens to us when we're done with this course?" Kelso demanded.

"You find a job. There's plenty of work. Company recruiters have more jobs than people. Most of 'em are pretty grim, but people do get rich on Mars, if they live long enough and find something they can do well. Most don't get rich, because the companies aren't in business to pay big salaries. And they know they've got your arse in a crack, because when that disk turns red you'll take the first offer you get. That's when they sign you up for ten-year contracts."

"Yeah, but—you mean we're just *loose?*" someone asked.

Farr laughed. "Yep. Whatever sentence you think you've got to serve, forget it. They don't give me a budget to run a prison and there are too many companies screaming for workers. Matter of fact, I erase the records when they come in. Nothing you ever did matters a damn now."

"How 'bout that?" There was a general babble. Some of the guys were laughing. "Son of a bitch, beat their asses again!" "Hell, thought I was facin' ten years in the bucket!" "But I really *am* a volunteer!"

"Now let me tell you about crime." Farr grinned. "Maybe some of you think you know something about the subject?"

He got a lot of laughs with that.

"You know nothing," Farr said. "We don't have much crime here. We live too close together to put up with people who steal from their comrades. Back on Earth you got busted, and maybe they sent you to court, and maybe they put you in the hands of the shrinks. You had parole officers, probation officers, social workers, welfare people, psychologists, and all that. Right?"

There were shouts. "Yeah."

"So they kept throwing you back until one day they lowered the boom on you," Farr was saying. "And they sent you here to work your balls off until a blowout kills you. That's the breaks. But before you think there's a better way than working, let me tell you that there's not one social worker on this whole planet."

He paused to let that sink in. "And we've got one jail in Hellastown. And no prisons. Or reform schools. Or detention hospitals. Or rehabilitation centers. Or *any* of that good crap. Give us trouble and we take off some hide. Give us more and we'll sell your contract to some awful place. Give us enough trouble and we put you outside. That's the way it is. You believe?"

Clear enough, I thought. I believed.

3

Survival training: pressure suits, because Mars has less than one percent of Earth's air pressure, and Farr wasn't kidding when he said the blood will boil in your veins. Air locks. Mining Equipment. Care of plants. Communications. Local customs, including knife fights and duels. This was taught by a Federation Marine corporal who told us we'd probably lose our first fight and not live to have any more. I think I could have taught him a couple of tricks, but he showed me some I'd never seen before.

There wasn't a hell of a lot to do but study. I figured the more I knew the better chance I'd have when they dumped us out, so I studied. Funny thing was, I found most of it pretty interesting. Before long I was glad of the longer Martian day. The clocks were standard twenty-four hours of sixty minutes each, but they had stuck into them an extra twenty-fifth "hour" of thirty-seven minutes just after midnight.

I was in a barracks with about thirty other men. The barracks room could have held five times that many. We'd been sent out on one of the smaller prison ships.

They gave us tests. All kinds. There were the funny games that shrinks like to play, and there were regular school-type tests as well. If you did well enough on the

24

tests, they gave you extra goodies, like chewing gum and lollipops. It sounds stupid, but if you don't have anything else, something as silly as a lollipop is worth working for. I worked.

The school was a funny place. It was taught by a one-legged man named Zihily. He drank himself to sleep every night and had hangovers in the mornings. He talked about whatever he felt like, no lesson plan or anything, and we had to get a lot of the information out of books, although he'd answer questions if you had any.

Zihily had a few words about those books. "You will find that those texts have been charged to you. Return them in good condition. If you do not, you will pay for them. They are very expensive. It takes a long time to work off that debt."

The whole place was like that. They told us what to do, but they didn't make us do it, and they didn't give a damn whether we did it or not. If fights started nobody stopped them unless the furniture got broken. Then the ones that did the breaking had to pay. Since they didn't have money, they paid by contracting labor. One guy owed two years already.

I came into the barracks one day to find Kelso fighting again, if you could call it a fight. He was holding a character up off the ground and slapping his face. I recognized a guy I privately called Snotty, who was a real dipshit. Kelso slapped him again.

"You like making trouble for people, don't you?" Wham.

"I didn't do anything to you!" Snotty whined.

"No, not to me." Wham. "But you thought it would be fun to tear up Lefty's books. Why did you think that would be fun?" Wham.

"Good enough, Kelso." We turned to see Hardesty, who was the guard sergeant in charge of our barracks. Hardesty wasn't a bad sort. He'd told us that if we kept the place clean and didn't break up the furniture he didn't give a damn what we did, and he pretty well meant it. He didn't hassle us much. "You can put him down now."

"He ripped up Lefty's books—" Kelso said.

"I know. He'll be charged for them. Lefty won't. I said, put him down, Kelso." There was an edge in Hardesty's voice.

"Okay."

"Let's go, Snowden," Hardesty said. "Off to see the Superintendent." Snowden was Snotty's real name. He was glad enough to get away from Kelso. They left the barracks. Snotty never came back. They sold him to a thorium mine somewhere south of us.

"Thanks, Kelso," Lefty said. He was a little guy, younger than me by maybe a year, and thin as a rail. Snotty wasn't much, but he could take Lefty apart. So could nearly anyone in the barracks.

"Glad to oblige," Kelso said.

Lefty had the bunk next to me. Later that night we got to talking. He claimed to be a volunteer, and maybe he was; there wasn't any way to tell. I knew there were a couple of genuine volunteers in the barracks because Hardesty told me so, but he didn't say which was which, and there probably weren't as many as claimed to be.

After that Lefty tended to hang around with me when he wasn't helping Kelso with his math. Lefty was pretty sharp with numbers, and he helped me sometimes when things got over my head. He was good at explaining, and God knows I needed somebody to talk to.

The chow wasn't very good, but there was plenty of it. Generally it looked and tasted like mush. The only good part was dessert: ice cream. You could have as much mush as you wanted, but you had to turn in your mush bowl to get dessert: one ice cream bar.

It was something to look forward to. Lefty and I ate together. One evening we'd got our dessert and went back to our seats in the chow hall.

"Chocolate," Lefty said. Then, like it was an after-thought, "Hal, what do you figure on doing when you get out of here?"

"I never thought. I hear the mines aren't much fun. And beginners have a high mortality rate." I didn't really like to think about it. In a way I liked the school. The lessons kept me busy, and I didn't have to worry about what to do. There was enough to eat, and after a couple of minor fights my barracksmates left me alone.

The only real lack was female companionship. Some of the others in the room were gay, but even the bad ones knew better than to be aggressive about it. There weren't any women in our room, and I didn't have any chance to get with the ones in the other barracks rooms, so the less thought about that the better. "I guess I'll just take what comes."

Lefty grinned. "I think we can do better than that. Want to throw in with Kelso and me?"

"In what?"

He reached into his pocket and came out with a pair of dice. He grinned broadly. "We'll do fine."

"Never saw you in the barracks games—"

"No point in it. Nobody's got anything to win. Out there, though—" He grinned again.

"Are you always lucky?" I asked.

"No luck to it. You watched those games? They take even money on sixes and eights. No way I can lose. Now if I can get into a game where there's some money—"

He didn't get to finish what he was going to say. A couple of hard cases from another barracks had come up behind me. I should have heard them, but I didn't. They didn't say a word. They just reached out and took the ice cream from out of our hands and walked off.

It sounds trivial. Who cares about a half-eaten ice cream bar? But when you've got nothing at all, the little you have is pretty important. Lefty was up and onto the nearest one with both fists.

They didn't even turn around. One of them put an elbow into Lefty's ribs. The other smashed him in the face. Lefty went down, and they looked at me. "Got anything to say about it?" the nearest one said.

"No." I made myself sound scared. "Nothing to say."

The guy grinned, and I kicked his kneecap in. If you get that right, the guy isn't going to do any walking for awhile. I didn't hit it perfect, but his leg buckled and he was off his feet. I moved away from him so he wouldn't be in the fight for a moment.

The other one came for me. He wasn't as big as I am, but he was ten years older. Sometimes that makes a lot of difference, even at twenty. He feinted with his hands and swung a kick to my head.

He was good at La savatte. I didn't have a chance to do anything but move with it so he didn't catch me very hard, but I acted stunned. The next kick he threw I was ready for and took his ankle, pushed it in the direction it was going already, and spun him right around. That let me get close enough to punch him in the crotch.

I don't like fights. When I was younger I swaggered a bit and started my share, but somewhere I lost the taste for that kind of thing. But if somebody does get me into it, I'm going to win if I can, and I don't care much about rules. When I saw this guy was out of action, I turned quick toward the one I'd kicked in the kneecap.

Sergeant Hardesty had hold of his collar. The guy could barely stand. "That'll do it," Hardesty said.

"Sure." I didn't figure they'd bother us again. One would limp for a week, and the other one looked like it would take a hydraulic jack to straighten him out before midnight.

"Your ice cream's all over the floor," Hardesty said. "Clean it up before you leave."

They said we weren't prisoners, but it was like a prison. We could go up to the dome in the evenings, but there wasn't a lot else to do. We didn't have any possessions, so there was nothing to gamble for. The few available women were booked solid. You could play cards, you could swap stories, and you could study.

I tried to get excited about being on Mars, but it didn't *seem* like Mars. I was getting used to the low gravity, and I'd stopped being amused over how far and how high I could jump. Except for the gravity we could have been in a cave on Earth.

Then we had p-suit training.

Zihily gave us no warning. He just announced that to-day would be it. "There are two types of pressure suits. The best fits only its owner. Obviously we have none of those for practice. The other variety is a general purpose Extra Vehicular Activity suit, commonly called a space suit, which will fit anyone of approximately the proper size. We have many of those. You will go out in parties of ten."

He called out ten names. Mine was not one of them. "You men will go out with Corporal Feinman for EVA suit training and practice."

They trooped off. They were laughing. They'd get to go outside, and it would be a break in the routine.

The rest of us listened to a lecture on mines and mining,

with emphasis on laser cutting tools, until the training party came back. There were only eight of them.

"What happened?" Zihily asked. He didn't sound very interested.

"Two of 'em didn't listen. We'll have to send out a party to get the suits back." Feinman sounded annoyed, and probably was. The suits were his responsibility.

I decided I would listen very carefully when my turn came.

* * *

"Super wants Pittson," the guard announced.

Zihily jerked a thumb toward the door. "Okay, Pittson, off you go."

I followed the guard out. Superintendent Farr's office was a large cubbyhole cut into rock. There weren't any windows, but where a window would be there was a big color holo of Mars as seen from Phobos. The desk was steel and glass, and the chairs were molded plastic. Farr sat behind his desk console typing inputs into a computer and looking up at the results as they read out on a screen above the desk.

The guard waved me inside. Farr didn't pay any attention until he'd finished whatever he was working on. Then he said, "Have a seat, Pittson. How are you?"

"Fine."

"You're pretty tough, aren't you?"

What was I supposed to say? "I don't know—"

"You put two men in sick bay and you don't know."

"They had it coming," I said.

"Didn't say they didn't. You're not in the rattle." He typed something else into the console. I couldn't see the results because the screen wasn't set where I could look at it. He studied it for a moment and said, "You've done pretty well in the school, too. You were in some kind of street gang back on Earth—"

"Yeah. I thought you erased those records."

"I do. But I look at them first. Were you a leader in that gang?"

"Kind of. Why?"

He ignored my question. "I thought so. Tell me, Pittson, what do you think of your classmates here?"

"Uh?" I thought about that. "I guess most of them are losers."

He nodded agreement. "Yes. There are only three main types who come here. There are failures, men who never amounted to anything back home and won't amount to anything here. Most of them don't last long. There are broken men who used to be important and can't stand the idea of starting over. And finally there are a few who can become Marsmen.

"Which are you?"

I shrugged. "I don't know."

"You'd better figure it out. You're about done here, Pittson. You've about finished the school—now what will you do?"

"I keep saying I don't know, but this time it's for damn sure I don't."

"What do you want to do?" he asked. He seemed very serious.

"I'd like to get out on my own, but there doesn't seem to be much chance of that. From what I've seen, your school tools us up to be company slaves!" I was getting a little mad at his routine. What was his angle, anyway?

He didn't react. Instead, he grinned. "Not a bad guess. Most pilgrims are. It's all the Federation will pay for, and it's all most of them could be. But there's opportunity on Mars, Pittson, if you're willing to work. And one day we'll have the Project going."

There was a far look in Superintendent Farr's eyes. He seemed to be seeing right through the rock walls of his office out onto the red, dusty surface of Mars; and he was looking at more than desert and sandstorms.

"The Project?" The capital letters had been obvious in his voice.

He shook his head as if clearing away cobwebs. "Yeah. There's a way to make Mars inhabitable. So you can live outside without a p-suit."

"You can do that?"

"We can do that. Marsmen can. But not now. The Federation Council won't put up the money. The company types want quick bucks. To hell with it, it's a dream. Maybe you will catch it one day. For now, I want you to tell me about yourself."

He was easy to talk to. I rambled on, and pretty soon

I was telling the story of my life. I was surprised at how much I said, and how personal it got. I suppose I shouldn't have been surprised, though; he was the first sympathetic listener I'd met since I was arrested, a hundred days and eighty million miles away in Baltimore's Undertown.

Finally he stopped me. "Are you willing to work?"

"Depends on the work."

"Reasonable. Suppose I tell you there's a job worth doing. Not company work, either. The big outfits aren't so bad, but what have you got with them? A salary at best. But what Mars needs is free men. Men who can tell the companies to roll it tightly and stuff it. Marsmen. Are you afraid of getting killed?"

"Well, sure, who isn't?"

"But you were in that gang war—"

"Yeah. It seemed like a good idea at the time."

He nodded. "Pittson, we're going to dump you out of here in a couple of days. When you're turned loose, go bum around downtown. Anybody asks you, you're waiting for a buddy. You don't have to say who, and don't. Just see what city life on Mars is like. And don't sign up with anybody until you've had an offer from some friends of mine."

"What kind of offer?" I was getting suspicious. What the *hell* was his angle?

"It'll be a good one. A chance to get out on your own, to be your own man. You'll work damned hard, but you'll have something to show for it. If you're good enough."

"How will I know it's them?" I asked.

"You'll know." Farr nodded to himself. "Now let me give you something else to think about. What do you have that's valuable?"

That didn't take much thought. "Nothing at all."

"Yes, you do. Your word. Is it good?"

I didn't understand and my face must have shown it. He shook his head and said, more to himself than to me, "It's an idea that's gone out of fashion on Earth. Out here a man's word is either good or it isn't. No compromises. Marsmen trust each other. We have to know that when a man gives his word he's not thinking about some way to weasel out.

"Pittson, nobody out here knows or cares what you did

before you got here. You can start over. You can be anything you want to be. Anything you're good enough to be and will work hard enough for. Now go think about that."

He waved dismissal and I left, wondering what it all meant. It was pretty heavy stuff for a guy my age and in my situation. I began to have some hope for the first time since—since I realized I wasn't going anywhere but Francis Scott Key Community College.

4

There wasn't any graduation ceremony. One morning after chow the speakers said, "REPORT TO CENTRAL PROCESSING" instead of announcing school call. It had been about a week since my interview with Farr. I had seen him only once since then, just passed him in the hall. He'd put his hand on my arm and winked at me, then hurried off.

It wasn't a lot to go on, but I'd built a lot of hope around Farr's promises. They were all I had, except for Lefty's offer, which I didn't think much of.

At Central Processing they charged our air tags to bright green, forty days' worth. They gave us a hundred Mars dollars, worth about half that in Federation credits. We changed our coveralls for new ones, with a choice of blue or orange.

Then they shoved us out the door. Literally—a big air-lock door. Fortunately the corridor beyond was pressurized. A hundred meters farther was another airtight door. Beyond that was Hellastown.

Hellastown was simply a lot more corridors and caves, with airtight doors at intervals so a blowout in one part wouldn't finish everybody. "Downtown" was a big five-story cavern, empty in the center. It was about half the size of a football field. It wasn't really all that big, but after the little caves and corridors of the school it looked huge.

All around the edges were openings to stores, offices, and cross-tunnels to other sections of the city. The cavern floor had been smoothed off and the holes filled in with that reddish concrete you saw everywhere on Mars. Above that were two more levels, the highest about seventy feet up. Two balconies ran around the cavern walls at the upper two levels. They had no rails, just a low wall about knee high.

On Earth some bureaucrat would have built a high fence to keep people from falling or jumping. Here nobody gave a damn.

One whole side of the square was lined with brothels, and there were lines outside each one. Everyone in the lines wore new coveralls. They seemed to be coming out about as fast as they went in.

"Son of a bitch!" Lefty yelled. "They'll spend all their money! Goddamn!"

"Uh—" Kelso pointed to the brothels. "It's been a long time—"

"We need a stake," Lefty said. "You don't want to blow it on that assembly line. Let's make some money and we'll buy a *real* lay."

"Yeah, well—" Kelso was undecided. Lefty went over to one of the lines. He started making a pitch for a dice game.

I drifted away from them. I thought about the brothels, because it had been a long time for me, too, but Lefty was right. There'd be no satisfaction in that, and my money had to last until I knew what to do next.

There were taverns, and I drifted into one. It was filled, partly with new-coveralled pilgrims, partly by men in dirty clothes and skintight underwear like Farr's. The beer was two bucks for a schooner. I looked longingly at it.

A dapper cat in creased coveralls was buying for a whole table of pilgrims. I watched as they poured it down. He beckoned for me to come join in, but I shook my head and stood, curious, because he had to have an angle and I didn't know what it was.

"You buying something or leaving?" the bartender yelled at me. He had one arm and one eye.

"Leaving, I guess," I said.

"Let him stay," somebody yelled. "Hey, kid, come have a drink." The guy was at a table with no pilgrims at all. He and seven others were pouring away the beer, and yelling stories at each other. "Come on, no hitch," he said.

I drifted over. He lifted a full schooner, drank half, and handed the rest to me. "Name's Andy Cernik," he said. "Sit down, smart pilgrim."

When I hesitated he laughed. "Go on, it's jake. No crimps here." He named the other people at the table, but I couldn't remember any of them. Two of the men were black, and another was Oriental. As I say, Federation policy goes in waves. They looked like they'd been on Mars for a long time.

"I'm Garrett Pittson," I said. "Crimps?"

Andy waved toward the table full of pilgrims. "Like Mister Sisson there. Your buddies'll wake up in the morning with a big head and a long hitch, wonderin' what happened to their bounty money. Hang around a couple of days, you'll get more choices."

"You guys miners?" I asked.

"Sure. Mars General. Not a bad outfit." They all laughed at some secret joke.

"What's it like in the mines?" I asked.

There was more laughing. "Goddamn hard, that's what," Andy said. "We lose maybe half the pilgrims their first year. But what the hell, it's a livin'. Could do worse."

"Sure," one of the black men said. "You could do worse by stickin' your head in a toilet maybe. Hard to think of another way."

They laughed and ordered another round. "Look, I can't pay," I told Andy.

"Yeah. Don't worry about it. Keep your stake; wish I had when they bounced me."

They didn't pay much attention to me after that. The brew was good, heavier and a lot more flavorful than Earthside beer. I found out the bartender owned the place and made the stuff himself. He'd been a Mars General miner in his day, which is why a lot of the MG crew came to his place.

35

The miners didn't seem to be a lot different from the Dog Soldiers: good men, tough and proud, but men with no place to go. They talked a lot about women they'd had, and which brothels were best, and how pilgrim day was the lousiest time to come to town, and how they wished the goddamn company would tell 'em when the Feddies were bouncing pilgrims so working stiffs could pick another day when the whores weren't slot-machining.

After a while somebody suggested they ought to look up an old buddy. I hoped they'd take me with them. I liked their company. But when they stood, Andy said, "See you around, Garr. If you sign up with MG, God help you, but look me up."

I went back out into the square. It wasn't like Earth at all, not topside and not Undertown. There were uniformed men I supposed were cops, but they didn't hassle anybody. The place was crowded, but not like downtown Baltimore, and except for us newcomers nobody was wandering aimlessly the way they do on Earth.

Another difference was that everyone carried a knife in plain sight. Some had big ones, broad-bladed things designed for combat and not much else. Others had smaller and more useful-looking sheath knives; but everybody was bladed. According to Zihily there were few guns on Mars, and the Federation people had them.

I saw a knife fight five minutes after I left the tavern.

Two men in blue coveralls, like ours but faded and patched, came out of a bar. They were shouting at each other. When they got outside they drew knives and squared off. A couple of cops drifted over, but they only stood and watched.

It started as a formal affair, with a lot of dodging and weaving, feints and counterfeints. They were good. Then the smaller guy made a tricky pass, thrusting up underhanded, and the big guy looked surprised as blood poured out of a gash in his lower arm.

"I'll be damned!" he said. He put his hand over the cut and drew away. "I will be dipped in dung."

"Probably."

"First blood enough?" a cop asked.

"Christ yes," the winner said. "Caz? Enough?"

"Oh hell yes." The loser looked at the cops. "I'll be at work tomorrow. No time lost."

The cop looked critically at the wound. "If you say so."
He looked to his partner and got a nod. "Okay."

"Right," Caz said. He looked at his bloody arm again.
"I will be dipped in crap."

"Probably."

They went back into the bar.

There were a lot of company offices around the main
square, places like Peabody, GE, Westinghouse, and the
other big outfits. The smaller companies had tables set up
in the open space. They were all pitching how wonderful
it would be to work for their outfits, but I noticed the
wages were low and about the same no matter where you
went.

Most of my classmates drank up their starter money,
signed on with a company, drank up their bounties, and
shipped off to work. They were gone within two days.

A few of us were still around. Lefty had a floating
crap game that he said was making food and air money
for himself and Kelso, and he was talking about opening
a gambling hall when they had a stake. I didn't see much
future in that, even if I'd been needed, which I wasn't.

Nobody cared about the dice games. Nobody cared
about anything that didn't cost labor time or get in the
way. I learned fast: you don't block the path of an armed
man, and you don't break up the furniture in bars. Neither lesson came the hard way for me; I learned from
another pilgrim's experience.

I found a tunnel end to sleep in. They'd been digging
out to expand the city, but this project was halted for
lack of a labor force. Nobody bothered me. I figured I
had nothing worth stealing, anyway. That turned out to
be stupid: I had a charged air tag, and that would be
worth my life if there was anybody around desperate
enough to cut my throat for it. Nobody was, just then.

Halfway between my tunnel end and the downtown
square was a store. It was quite literally a hole in the wall,
owned by a man who'd been crippled in the mines. His
buddies had chipped out a couple of rooms for him, and
he sold food, beer, water, and anything else he could buy
cheap and sell later. He gave me a runner's job, going to
the bakery for stale bread to feed his chickens, carrying
chicken droppings to the recycling works, running across

town to deliver beer to some old friend who gave him business out of charity. The wages were simple: two hours work for a meal with beer, and he wouldn't pay my air taxes. It was hardly a permanent job.

Everything was expensive. It cost more if it came in a can. In fact, cans were worth as much as what was in them, and some scraggly kids made a living cruising the tunnels looking for miners' beer parties where they might get thrown a can or two.

After a couple of days old Chad trusted me enough to let me sleep in the store. I worked pretty hard for him, straightening up the store and chipping out some new shelves in the rock. He needed that done, but he didn't have the tools, and he was too stove in to do it with hammer and chisel and too broke to buy plastic shelving.

I finished a little niche, not one hell of a lot accomplished for all that work. He drew a beer from his barrel and handed it to me. "Garr, I can use the help, but what are you waitin' for? I can't pay your air taxes, and that tag's going to start turning color."

"Yeah, I know. Man said to wait for a friend of his."

"You give your word?"

"Sort of."

"He give his?"

"Yeah," I said.

"Good man?"

I thought about that. Was Farr a good man? I wanted him to be. "I think so."

Chad nodded gravely. "Then you wait, that's all. It'll be okay. If something's happened, though, maybe my buddies can fix you up with a short hitch at Peabody. It's not a bad outfit, as outfits go."

I went back to chipping rock. It wasn't as hard as granite, but it wasn't soapstone either. It was red like everything else. "Mars anything like you expected?" Chad asked.

"Well, they kept saying on Earth that Mars was a frontier. I guess I expected it to be like the old western movies . . . "

"Is, lots of ways."

"Maybe." I laid down the hammer and took another slug of beer. "But you can't get out on your own. Can't live off the land."

"Farmers do."

"Sure, with a hundred grand worth of equipment—"

"Don't take that much. Work for a good outfit, save your wages, the banks will put up a lot of it if you've saved a stake. Ten years work, maybe, if you save your money. Then you're out of here. That's how most of the Rimrats got started. Wish I'd done it. Can't, now."

I thought about it. When you're twenty, ten years is a long time. Half your life. But there sure didn't seem much future hanging around here. "If this other deal doesn't come through, maybe I'll do that," I said. "Only I wonder if I can save the money—"

"That's the blowout for most, all right," Chad said. "You just stick tight a couple of days, though."

"Sure, you need the help—"

"Aah, there's that too, but maybe things'll work out better'n you expect."

"Sure." But I didn't have much hope of it. A man's word is either good or it isn't, Farr had said. It looked like his wasn't. Why had I expected anything different from a prison warden?

I'd been there ten days and my air tag was turning from green to yellow. It was getting time to move on. I figured another couple of days would do it.

A big man came into the store. He wasn't as big as Kelso, and he was a lot older, but there was nothing small about him. "Ho, Chad," he called. Then he saw me and looked me over, slowly, in a way I didn't like.

Chad came out of the other room. "Sarge Wechsung," he said. "Figured you'd show up one of these days." Chad looked at me about the way Sarge had. "Come for the kid?"

"Yeah. Pittson, I had a hell of a job runnin' you down. Old Man said to look you up next time I was in town. Had some trouble gettin' here."

"The Old Man? Oh, you mean Superintendent Farr—"

"Sure." They both talked at once, cutting me off, as if they didn't want me to say the name.

"I hear you're looking for a job," Wechsung said. "I got one. Come on, let's go, I'm runnin' out of time." His voice was raspy, as if he'd been used to shouting a lot. It didn't sound particularly friendly.

"Just where are we going?" I asked.

"I got a station out on the Rim. Windhome. Nobody watchin' the place, got to be gettin' back. Need a farm-hand. You'll like it. Work your arse off, do you some good. Right, Chad?"

"Damn right," the old man said. He rubbed his crippled leg. "Wish you'd been around when I come here. Go on, Garrett. He's a good man."

Take the word of a man I didn't know about a man I'd just met. Well, what the hell, I thought. What have I got to lose?

A lot.

"Let's go, let's go, got to get you outfitted," Wechsung said. "Chad, we'll be down at Smitty's place if you want to send down some lunch—"

"Send how? You're stealin' my runner. I'll bring it my-self."

"Right." Wechsung walked out. He didn't look back to see if I was following.

I stood there a moment, then caught up with him.

5

The suit was a tight bodystocking of an elastic weave, with metal threads running through it that fitted like it had been painted on. The outfitter chewed gum and made stupid jokes about blowouts while he literally built the suit around me. He cut the cloth, stretched it, and heat-welded the plastic threads while it was in place. Then I took off that part and he finished the welding job. When it was all done it fit snugly, not quite tight enough to cut off circulation, and looked something like a thin version of a skin diver's wet suit.

"We first came here, they didn't have thread that would stand up," the outfitter said. "This new stuff's great, though. You can gain maybe five kilos and it'll still fit. Don't put on more weight than that, though, or you'll be buying a new suit."

The pressure suit ended with a gasket at the neck. A helmet dogged onto that. With pressure in the helmet you could go outside. The skintight bodystocking reinforces your own skin so it can take the internal pressure, and your sweat glands are the temperature regulator. Marsmen wear skintights everywhere because if there's a blowout and you get your helmet on quick, you may stay alive.

That was quite a helmet, with lights, a radio, and hoses

meant to connect to air tanks. The tanks went in a back-pack. There was more to the outfit: reflective coveralls, heavy foam-insulated jacket and trousers, thick gloves, a tool kit that snapped onto a belt, boots, a knife, and another radio in a holster.

Smitty the outfitter had set up a table outside for people waiting while he worked on their gear. Chad brought lunch and beer.

"Doesn't this cost a lot, Mr. Wechsung?" I asked.

"Call me Sarge. Sure it costs."

I didn't understand and I guess my face said so.

"Think you're not worth it? Hell of a time to tell me. Once Smitty starts cuttin', I've bought it."

I didn't say anything, and he laughed. It was a cheerful laugh. He didn't sound worried about anything, but I knew it would take more than a year for me to save up what he was paying. "Let us worry about the costs," he said. He looked around. No one was listening to us. "The Skipper thinks you might make a Marsman, and I take the Commander's word for it."

"You mean Mr.—"

"Yeah."

Commander. That squared with the black bands on Farr's coverall sleeves. "Are you still in the Federation Service?" I asked.

"Hell no. Retired years ago. So did the Old Man. He went to prisoner chasin' and I went to farming. What do they call you, Pittson?"

"Garrett's my name—"

"Fine. Garrett, you were told to think about something. Did you?"

"Yes."

"And?"

"I'll make my word good."

Sarge grinned. "Okay. And you can trust people, a little anyway, or you wouldn't have waited for me. Garrett, I have a big place out there. Lots of work. You'll sweat your balls off, and I won't pay you much, but you stick with me a Mars year—that's two Earth years—and you'll know the score and have a stake you can use to get out on your own. That's what you want, right?"

"I think so—"

"What anybody in his right mind wants."

Chad shuffled up to collect the beer mugs. Across the square a group of miners came out of a brothel. They were laughing and shouting as they got onto the jitney that would take them back to their barracks.

"What happened to the last man you had helping you?" I asked.

"Got his own place. A couple of dozen have come through Windhome, Garrett. Some got themselves killed. Some couldn't stick it and ran back here to work for a company outfit. But five have their own stations."

"And why are you doing this?"

Sarge shrugged. "You ask too many questions. Finish your beer. Your stuff's about ready and we've got to move before sundown. The tractor won't run so good in the dark."

The tractor wouldn't run at all in the dark. It had solar cells all over it—on the roof, on the decks in front and behind the passenger compartment, and on wings that could fold up when it was inside but unfolded when it was running. The solar cells furnished all the power.

It was very comfortable. The passenger compartment was bigger than I had expected and had a bunk as well as seats. This was the only pressurized part of the tractor; the rest would seal up to keep out dust, but if you had to carry cargo under pressure you put it in airtight bags.

Sarge drove up the ramp from inside the city. It went up steeply, a dark tunnel with a few lights. There were three sets of air locks at the top. Then we were outside. The sun was high in the west; it seemed very bright after my time in Hellastown.

When we got onto the plains, the motors whined as the solar cell wings extended. "Okay, watch what I do," Sarge said. "Now we're outside we switch from batteries to direct solar power. This thing develops about fifty horsepower, enough to move pretty fast and still keep the batteries charged in full sun, but you don't want to run at night. It won't go more than a couple of hours."

I looked around at the Marscape. It was bleak, and in two minutes we were out of sight of Hellastown. We drove through fields of boulders. They came in all types, from house-sized to just rocks. Red dust blew all around. "What happens if you're caught out at night?" I asked.

"You pray of lot." Sarge nodded to himself. "Pray a lot and hope your air lasts. Then curl up and go to sleep. Batteries should give enough heat to last the night. It gets cold out there."

About a hundred below zero, I remembered from the school. But in summer daytime it was warm enough to go out without a jacket, as long as you had a p-suit and air.

"The manuals for the tractor are in that compartment," Sarge said. "When we get home, take 'em inside and read up."

"Sure."

"And don't forget to put 'em back before one of us has to use Aunt Ellen again."

"Aunt Ellen?"

"The tractor. Next to your p-suit, a tractor's the most important thing in your life. Treat Aunt Ellen right and she'll take care of you."

A strong wind was blowing outside. Hellas is a low basin, formed a billion years ago when a rock the size of Greenland smashed into Mars. The impact melted the rock, and lava flowed up from inside Mars to cover the hole. Huge chunks of rock were thrown up into a rimwall, and more rocks were thrown out to make another ring of secondary craters around that.

Then for the next billion years Hellas and the Rim were pounded by smaller meteoroids. They left the basin flat but partly covered with junk. Since there weren't any hills, the visibility was terrible; we were lost in a jungle of rocks. The wind whipped the dust around so thick we could hardly see out.

"You're crazy, you know," I said.

"How's that?"

"You don't know a damn thing about me. Superintendent Farr talked to me for maybe three hours—"

"Best not mention that when anybody else is around."

"Yeah, but—"

"We have the test results, Garrett Psych and skills both. And maybe we've kept an eye on you better than you know."

"You still don't know I'm not planning to murder you for the tractor!"

Sarge laughed. "What would you do with it? Everybody knows it's mine. And just how long would you live out here?"

"Yeah." I watched the dust for a moment. "They taught us just enough, didn't they? Just enough to know there's a lot they didn't tell us."

Sarge grinned. It was a nice grin. "See how smart you're gettin' already? Know any good songs?"

He knew a lot more of them than I did. We sang along to pass the time.

"You got to learn more songs," he complained. "Here, let's teach you 'The Highland Tinker.' We'll work up to 'Eskimo Nell'— Hey! Look, over there. See it?"

I looked where he pointed. "Nothing I see."

"Gone now. Sand cat, maybe."

I looked at him to see if he was putting me on. He didn't look like it. "An animal? There aren't any animals on Mars!"

"That's what the books say. Me, I'm not so sure. Every now and then you see something moving. Just a flash. Some say they've seen 'em close up, about the size of a squirrel, red brown, blends with the sand."

"I thought animals weren't even possible. No air."

"Yeah." Sarge grinned again. "I'm not sayin' those who've seen 'em close up hadn't had a few. Still in all, it's a big planet and there's a lot about it we don't know."

"That's for sure." And there are plants, I thought. Plants that have the biologists climbing the walls, because they're kin to Earth lichens and can even crossbreed with some Earth strains, but they aren't the same at all. Mars plants cover themselves with a glass bubble like snail shell but more transparent.

"Wonder what'll happen to 'em?" Sarge said.

"To who?"

"To the sand cats. When we get the Project goin', can the goddamn cats live after there's air? But they do say Mars has had air before, so maybe they can. Hope so."

"Tell me about this project. Commander Farr mentioned it, but I haven't heard much from anybody else."

Sarge guided the tractor around a boulder. "The Project's a plan, a way to pump the atmosphere up to maybe a tenth Earth normal, maybe more, enough so we can go outside without p-suits. Warm the planet up. Green things growing, not just in domes, all over."

45

"Won't that take a long time?"

"Maybe. Not as long as you'd think, the way they tell me. Only we can't get started. Earth bastards won't let us."

We went over a ramp. This road had been used before, if you could call it a road. The only way I knew was here and there boulders had been blasted apart, or there were ramps over some of them. We topped a ramp and I got a good view of the plain and the blowing dust.

"One of these days we'll do it ourselves," Sarge said. "Only it takes things we don't have. Like atom bombs."

I shuddered. Like everyone else on Earth I had been brought up to think of atom bombs as something to kill worlds with. I said that.

"Just tools, Garrett. Just tools. We need the bombs to trigger volcanoes. There's a lot more air and water inside this planet if we can get them out. Then it'll come alive."

We topped another ramp and Sarge stopped the tractor. Without the whine of the electric motors it seemed very quiet, but then I heard the wind, howling ceaselessly, and the crackle as it blew sand against the tractor.

There was nothing out there but dust and the distant mountains. It didn't look as if it had ever been alive, or ever would be. Nothing moved but dust forming into little twisters that Sarge called dust devils.

We were utterly alone. If we got into trouble nobody was around to help us, and we'd have to get out by ourselves or not at all.

Well, I'd wanted to be on my own. I'd got that.

6

A hundred days went by. There were a lot of times when I wished I hadn't come, and twice I was ready to leave, but talked myself out of it.

We sat in the little bubble-dome at the end of a corridor into Windhome. Sarge called it his veranda. Since the dome was a hundred meters above the floor of Hellas Basin, we had a view that stretched for miles, but there wasn't a lot to see except boulders and dust devils.

Inside the dome we had a jungle of plants, and hard chairs. In Mars' low gravity you don't really need cushions anyway. I hoisted my beer and waved it at Sarge. "You weren't kidding when you said you'd work my arse off!"

"Right."

Down below, the agricultural co-op tractor snaked across the basin floor. It pulled six trailers of produce from stations along the Rim. A lot of it was ours.

That had been the first fight I'd had with Sarge: he was desperate to get production higher and higher, make bigger and bigger profits, and I couldn't understand why we couldn't take it easy and relax. There'd be plenty to eat without all that work.

"Sure," he'd said. "But how do I pay the taxes?"

"Taxes?"

"Federation bastards tax hell out of us."

47

There was another reason he wanted profits, but I didn't find that one out until later.

Now I sat drinking beer. It was slightly sour and I thought I knew a way to improve it. I'd been studying the tapes from the central library, and had the notion that Sarge was using the wrong malting process, one designed for big breweries with better equipment than we had. I'd found a taped copy of an old book, published in 1895, that told how they did it back then and I wanted to try it.

"Drink up," Sarge said. "We got a lot more to do before we turn in."

"Right." I was in no hurry. The work was never finished, but we were caught up for a while. We'd spent the day harvesting corn and wheat from our hydroponics tanks out in the big glass agro-domes. It had been a lot of work. Now it was getting dark out, and we wouldn't be able to work in the domes any more—so we'd do inside maintenance.

There wasn't enough power to do heavy work at night because Windhome ran on solar cells just like the tractor. Closer to Hellastown there were stations drawing power from the nuclear plant, but not out here on the Rim.

I watched the last of the sunlight. There aren't any sunsets on Mars. There's either light or there isn't, for the same reason that shadows are so dark in the daytime: no atmosphere to diffuse the light and make a bright sky like Earth's. On Mars you can be in pitch-black shadow a few feet from bright sunlight.

"You been studying that problem?" Sarge asked.

"Yeah. We can do it. These solar cells are mostly grown crystal, and the circuits to control the growth aren't that tough. Give me the right materials and we'll grow our own."

"Save a lot of money," Sarge said. "Glad you're up on that electronics bit. I never had the time to study it. Doesn't make much sense to me anyway."

I doubted that. I never saw a problem Sarge Wechsung couldn't solve if he had to. Anyway, the library has most of it laid out cookbook style. You just have to be careful to look up all the words, because what an engineer means by a word isn't always the same as what other people mean.

"You said you'll need germanium," Sarge said.

"Right. We don't have any."

"None I've found. Sam Hendrix does though, and he's only about forty kilometers from here."

That made him a near neighbor. Our nearest had a station twelve kilometers away, but I'd never met him except on the phones. I hadn't met Hendrix, either.

"We'll have to run over and buy some," Sarge said. He sat and watched dust devils for a moment. "Sorry you came, kid?"

"No." I was surprised at how easy it was to answer that. It hadn't been the easiest time of my life.

A week before I'd had a blowout. Sarge had given me Number Three agro-dome to plant whatever I wanted. I'd put in tomatoes and squash and nursed them along until they were almost ready to harvest. Then, while I was mixing nutrients for the hydroponic food system, the join between the glass dome and the bedrock below had gone.

Pressure went to nothing in a couple of seconds. I panicked, but remembered to yell to get the air out of my lungs so I wouldn't explode. Then I got control of myself, looked around for my helmet, found it, and dogged it onto the neck seal of my suit. I closed the face plate and reached down to the air valves, bringing air pressure into my suit. Ten seconds later I was back under pressure. You'd be surprised just how long ten seconds can be.

Then I got the shakes. Sarge had drilled me in blowout practice every day since we came. Anytime he might shout "Blowout!" and if I took more than ten seconds to find my helmet and get it on, he'd make life pure hell. I was damned glad of the practice now.

Tomatoes and squash had exploded all over the dome. Sarge was inside less than a minute after it happened. He came as quick as he could, but if I hadn't taken care of myself, he'd have been too late. We stood there and looked at the wreckage of my crop. The leaves had already wilted—everything in the dome was dead. Everything except me. We got the dome patched that afternoon and I was planting again the next day.

I'd had a blowout, I'd had screaming fights with Sarge, I'd had the blue funks from looking at that blue, bright dot near the sun, I'd worked my arse off, and I had no money at all. "No. I'm not sorry I came."

"Glad to hear it. You do good work. We make enough profit, I can outfit you earlier than I thought."

I will be dipped in shit, I thought. So that's why he grinds so hard at it. "Thanks. Uh—Sarge?"

"Yeah?"

"One thing. Are we ever going to see any women?"

"Oh yeah." He gave me that big booming laugh of his. "I thought I worked you hard enough to keep the urges under control—"

"I'll never work *that* hard."

"Yeah, well, couple of weeks, no more'n a month."

"Oh. When we go back to town."

"Naw, not them whores. We're farmers, not labor clients. Hang on a while, kid. You'll see. You're just getting started out here."

"That's for sure." I looked at my hands. They were calloused and had the red dust of Mars ground into them. I was drinking sour beer, and my ear hurt from the blowout. There was a small network of veins coming to the surface on my right cheek, also a result of the blowout, and I knew I had enough work to fill three or four hours before I could go to bed. Tomorrow morning we'd be up at dawn to start cutting a new tunnel.

I felt terrific. I knew where I was going, and I had a friend to rely on. I wasn't a pilgrim any more.

* * *

We had the tractor loaded, and I went to the passenger side of the cab.

"Nope. You drive," Sarge said.

I shrugged and went around to the other side and we got strapped in. I wondered what to do next. Two dozen assorted dials, switches, and controls stared up at me. I looked to Sarge for advice, but he'd curled up in his seat and closed his eyes.

I'd studied the training manuals, and Sarge had checked me out. Now's as good a time for a solo as any, I told myself. Here goes. I hit the switch to activate the control panel and began the checklist.

Doors sealed. Begin pressurization, and watch the gauge. Also keep an eye on the balloon and see that it flattens out; gauges have been wrong before. Pressure to seven pounds a square inch, half Earth normal.

Sarge reached up and undogged his face plate. He still hadn't opened his eyes.

I went on through the list. Battery power on. Activate the garage doors. Back her out, slow, there's no steering wheel, there's two clutches and throttles, and if we ram something we can blow out. Or worse. We crawled out into the bright Martian sunshine. Extend the solar cell wings. Switch to direct power. Get the course off the map.

"Damn!" I'd forgotten to calibrate the gyrocompass. Mars' magnetic field isn't reliable enough for navigation. Sarge was still pretending to be asleep.

I took a bearing on a distant peak, got a reading off the map, and lined the tractor up. I looked it over again, and everything seemed right, so I set the compass to the bearing and hit the calibration switches. It locked in, and I slewed Aunt Ellen around onto the course laid out on the map.

"Pretty good," Sarge muttered. "Wake me up if you need to and don't take her more than twenty klicks an hour."

Then I think he really did go to sleep.

Aunt Ellen wasn't as hard to drive as I'd thought she would be, and after a while I had the knack of it. I drove east along the base of the Rim, watching where I was going rather than looking at the scenery. Two hours later we were there.

"Ice Hill," Sarge said. "Sam Hendrix's place. It'd be better if you didn't say anything about germanium."

I grinned. I'd heard Sarge dicker with his neighbors over the phone. Listening to him you got the impression he had plenty of what he needed to buy and none of what he had to sell.

Like Windhome, Hendrix's station had no real form above ground, just seemingly random protrusions onto the face of Hellas Rim. But Ice Hill was a lot larger than Windhome, with over a dozen glass agro-domes, at least two bubble verandas on balconies high up on the side of the Rim, and two separate garage ramps. A dozen people milled around outside the station. To me, by now, that was a big crowd.

Suddenly one member of the crowd was different. Strange. Graceful. I stared—

"Yep," Sarge said. "Her name's Erica. Sam's number two daughter. Oldest one's married off already. Uh, Garrett—"

"Yeah?"

"Go easy. The Hendrix clan's tough, and they've got some strong prejudices."

"You mean don't seduce the daughters—"

"I mean make sure it's seduction you got in mind, and not something more forceful. Otherwise don't be too surprised if you find a knife up against your ribs."

"Hmm. Maybe I better stick with the whores."

"They're safer," Sarge said. "For the short haul, they're safer."

We entered the cleared area near the main ramp into Hendrix's pressurized garage. Windhome's garage area wasn't sealed; when we needed to work on Aunt Ellen we had to haul her into the main shop.

"They won't mind if I *talk* to the ladies, will they?" I asked.

"Christ, Garrett, don't make a big thing out of it."

"Don't make a big thing, but be careful?" I said.

"Yeah, something like that. Sorry I mentioned it."

The air-lock door opened and I guided the tractor up the ramp.

"One thing," Sarge said. "I can understand you gettin' a little excited over the prospect of female company, but I'd fold up the wings 'fore I took the tractor through that door, was I you."

Sam Hendrix was waiting for us in the garage; before Sarge could tell him my name he started talking politics. Hendrix was a wiry fellow, a bit over fifty, with steel-gray crew-cut hair, a bristly mustache, and a big scar running down his left cheek. He had some kind of accent, but too faint for me to place it.

"There is a new administrator in Hellastown. They say there will be a new charter as well. Have you heard?" he demanded.

"Reckon I've heard something about it," Sarge told him. "Sam, this is my new buddy. Garrett Pittson. Good man."

"I'm glad to meet you. Welcome to our home. Sarge,

they are talking about raising taxes again. Again! Not for the big companies. Only for us. How will we live? Ah, I am forgetting my manners. Perry, show these people to their rooms. Dinner is in one hour. Glad to have met you, Garrett Pittson." He talked that way, a mile a minute, without much pause between thoughts.

Perry looked about eight Earth years old, a nephew or grandson or something. He was already wearing a pressure suit. I thought it must be pretty expensive to keep buying p-suits for kids as they grew out of them. Perry led us through a maze of twisting corridors and up some stairs. We exited into a big cavern that was the main hall, big enough to hold a hundred people or more, then walked across to another stairway. Ice Hill was a *lot* bigger than Windhome.

There were twenty people at dinner. I sat across a narrow table from Erica Hendrix. Her big brother Michael was next to me. Mike was married and had two kids already. He lived in a separate part of the Hendrix complex.

I must have talked with Mike and the others during dinner, but I don't remember any of it. I kept looking across at Erica. She had long red hair that she'd had up in braids when I first saw her; she put it up for outside work. For dinner she'd let it down in waves that reached her shoulders. It was a deep copper red, not like the color of Mars dust. She had bright blue eyes and a pointed nose. She was a big girl, not a Ukrainian tractor driver type, but big and well proportioned.

I thought she was the most beautiful woman I'd ever seen in my life. I couldn't take my eyes off her even to eat. I think I embarrassed her, but I couldn't help it. I kept telling myself that any girl would look good just now, but I knew better.

Dinner was a huge affair. Hendrix kept pigs and cattle as well as chickens, so there was real meat, and milk, and cheese, as well as fresh vegetables and bread and *pudding*. Also, they kept the pressure higher than we did, enough so you could get the *smells* of the food as well as the taste. It was marvelous. We didn't eat like that at Windhome.

The prettiest girl I'd ever seen and the best meal I'd

ever eaten. I kept telling myself it was the contrast from what I was used to. Maybe. But it was a great dinner.

Erica was my age, almost to the day. Since she'd been born on Mars it took some figuring to be sure of that. Her brother fished out his computer to check on it. Neither of them knew much about Earth's calendar—they thought all the months had the same number of days—and I had trouble with Mars' calendar with those extra intercalary days. The Martian year isn't quite two Earth years long, and has 24 months, plus extra days. It was fun figuring out what day it was on Earth when she was born.

Everybody worked at the Hendrix place. The kids served dinner and cleaned up afterward. Clearly the women regarded the kitchen work as their special preserve, but not all of them worked there. Erica, for instance, took care of an agro-dome and did power plant work on the side. Her mother said she had better marry a good cook.

There were drinks after dinner, then finally the various subgroups of Hendrixes melted away, leaving Sam, Erica, Sarge, and myself. Sam invited us into what he called his office, which was a comfortable-looking chamber about twenty feet square filled with all kinds of odds and ends he'd made or collected. He got down a bottle of brandy and poured a shot for each of us. Erica tossed hers off like water but didn't want a second.

"Guess we ought to do some talking," Sarge said. "No point in them havin' to listen. You reckon Erica could show Garrett around? I'd like him to see what a real station looks like."

"Certainly, why not?" Hendrix said. As we left, Sam was saying, "Now this new administrator will be a problem. And they have brought in two companies of Federation Marines, did you know that? I tell you Sarge, it is getting thick."

There didn't seem to be anybody around. Since the sun was down the station was on batteries for the night, and most of the lights were off. The corridors were lit by little pools of light separated by deep-shadowed stretches.

"We're a bewilderin' lot, aren't we?" Erica demanded. She was laughing at me. I didn't mind. It was a nice laugh.

"Well, there are a lot of you," I said.

She grinned. "Father, two uncles, Uncle Ralph's wife's brother and his family, Michael and his wife and her brother—you were funny, tryin' to remember all the names. Have you been with Sarge Wechsung for long?"

"Five months. This is the first time we've left Windhome since I got there."

"They say Sarge works his recruits pretty hard."

"He does that."

"It doesn't last forever, though," she said. "Have you thought about where you'll want your own station?"

"No—we haven't talked about that much."

"But you do want a place of your own?"

"Sure. That's what makes all the work go easy."

She laughed at that. I loved that laugh. Poets talk about laughs like that one. "Wish something would make it easy for me! All of Sarge's people, the ones that stuck with it, have pretty good stations. You'll get yours." She led me through more corridors. The station was big, and I wondered about the air supply. It would take a lot to keep that large a volume under pressure—and they kept it higher than we did.

"We've hit lots of ice," Erica said. "More than a cubic kilometer of permafrost."

That explained it. With that much ice they didn't have to bother about recycling; with solar power, water can be broken into hydrogen and oxygen. Save the hydrogen for fuel if you've got extra oxygen to burn it in—or chemical processing, or even throw away the hydrogen; it won't matter. You've got the essential part of air. Water and sunlight and oxygen, all Hendrix would ever need. That's the nice thing about planets, and the reason the space colonies never succeeded: there's nothing out there in space, nothing to mine and nothing to prospect.

"We have enough to last a thousand years," she said. "Although the way Dad keeps expandin' this place—"

As we laughed she led me up a ramp and then we were on a flight of stairs leading to another tunnel. I was thoroughly lost. "There's a nice valley on the other side of the ridge from here," she said. "Make a good station. Ice there, I think. The Rim's getting crowded, all the way from Hellastown to Big Rock Candy."

Crowded. The closest stations were seven or eight kilometers apart. Crowded. Of course she was right: the best claims, with ice and good mining, were all taken.

There was a small, airtight door at the end of the tunnel. She automatically checked the gauge for pressure on the other side—I was learning that habit, but she'd grown up with it—then opened it and we went through.

We stood a hundred meters above the Hellas Basin floor. There were flickering lights in some of the station's agro-domes down below. Phobos was almost overhead. Phobos is only about a twentieth as bright as Luna, but that's enough to show the basin floor and the rocks piled along the Rim. The little moon zips right along. You can't quite see it move, but if you look away a minute and look back you can see it isn't in the same place.

"Pretty out there," Erica said. "What's it like to stand outside under the moon, with no pressure suit?"

I tried to tell her about Earth, and about warm nights and soft breezes. I told her about going to the ocean at night. She had never seen an ocean and never would. Of course she'd read about them, but she didn't know, and I found myself getting homesick and choked up when I tried to tell her about all the things Earth has that we'd never see on Mars. Oceans and forests and whales and elephants and—

"Someday we'll have forests," she said. "And we'll go outside without these suits." Her eyes shone.

"So you're a Project nut too."

"Aren't you?"

"Don't know enough about it," I said. That was a mistake; I got an engineering dissertation. I liked her voice, and if necessary I'd have listened to her recite bad poetry in a language I didn't know, but a lecture on the Project wasn't the topic I'd had in mind for a tête-à-tête under the hurtling moons of Barsoom (actually, Deimos wasn't up yet, but never mind) with the most beautiful girl in the universe.

And yet. Maybe it was earlier, maybe it was just then, while she told me about how it would be some day when there was air on Mars and it stayed warm all night in summer, and there would be green fields and forests— maybe then, maybe earlier, but I knew as well as I knew anything that this was the girl I wanted to marry.

Crap, I told myself. Garrett, you haven't seen any women for months. Anybody you met just now would be the One and Only, which is a bunch of romantic claptrap you don't believe in in the first place.

Maybe so, I answered myself. But I've known a lot of girls, and I never felt like *this* before, and damned good it feels, too.

What you need, Garr baby, is a trip to Hellastown.

Go away. The idea is nauseating.

"We'll do it," she said. "We'll make Mars green and beautiful, the way Earth is, and it will be ours."

"Earth isn't—" I couldn't finish it. Earth *is* green and beautiful, except where people have messed it up.

We must have talked for another hour, but I don't remember what about. Finally I got up the nerve to reach for her hand. She didn't draw back. Well, here goes, I thought. I drew her to me and kissed her.

That went on for quite a while. Then she pushed me away. "I'm no expert on this, but I think we'd better stop," she said.

"Why?"

"Because I've got the feeling we stop now or we don't stop at all—"

"And why stop at all?"

"I just think we'd better." She moved away from me and perched on a bench on the other side of the small dome. "Garrett, I am not a town girl—"

"Lord, I never—"

"Let me finish. I live on the Rim. I like it here. I know that girls in town, not whores, just girls, have plenty of affairs, and they must enjoy them. I'm damned sure I would. But then what? I intend to live on the Rim. I don't think I could stand it in town. But stations are family affairs, and I do not believe I want to get involved with anyone I'm not going to live with for a long time."

"And I'm a convict and—"

"Oh, shut up. You're just past being a pilgrim. In about a year you'll have a stake and when that time comes, if we can still stand the sight of each other, we'll open this conversation again. Until then, no."

"Yeah. Okay. I'm sorry."

"What's there to be sorry about? Didn't you enjoy it? I certainly did. I know I don't have much experience at this sort of thing, but you didn't seem too bored at the time. Now I think we ought to go downstairs, because I have work to do in the morning."

7

"Thinking about Erica? Pretty girl," Sarge said.

I concentrated on guiding the tractor around a small crater. The wind had come up, and whipped the dust in our faces so that visibility was bad. When I could look up, I threw Sarge a grin. "Well, actually I was thinking about the trees."

"Sure you were."

"Well, I *was*. Just then, anyway."

We both laughed. "You know, Garr, I've been meaning to grow some fruit trees myself one of these days. Fruit trees make sense. But you know what Ruth Hendrix wants? A wood table for the dining room."

Erica had told me that, but I wasn't going to spoil Sarge's story.

"Yep, a wood table," Sarge said. "Be the only goddamn piece of wood furniture on Mars. Tax collectors ever saw a thing like that, they'd break old Sam. Dah! Why'd I get on that subject?"

"Why would the tax collectors care what Sam's table is made of?" I asked.

"Property tax." Sarge snorted in contempt. "Otherwise known as a fine for improving your property. You've got a lot to learn about Mars politics, and I guess you ought to start now. The Federation runs Mars to suit the big companies."

"The only thing I've seen the Federation in charge of was the prison ship and the school—"

"Yeah. Well, the school's Commander Farr's idea. He runs it in a way that helps us out. But the rest of it's Earth types, bureaucrats, don't want anybody to get ahead. And they're bringing in marines to make sure."

"You used to be a Federation Marine."

"Sure." Sarge sniffed his contempt. "Old style. We were peace keepers, back when keeping the peace on Earth was a damn dangerous job. None of my type left. The new marines are bloody thieves in uniform, out for wages and what they can steal. That's why the Skipper retired. He wanted no part of being a tax collector!"

"What do they do with the money they collect?"

Sarge laughed. "They don't put it to anything that helps us, you can be damned sure of that! Be different if they'd finance the Project, but not them." His voice changed to an unctuous whine. "Mister Speaker, we cannot destroy the ecology of an entire planet! To humans, perhaps, a breathable atmosphere on Mars is desirable, but to Mars it is no more than pollution . . . I swear to God, kid, I heard one of the goddamn Federation Councilors say that!"

I shook my head. "Sam grows the trees and makes the table. Why should the Federation take a cut for that? It's not very fair."

"Yeah. Question is, what do we do about it?"

"What can we do?" I asked.

He didn't answer. Instead, he sat up and rubbed his eyes, then said, very slowly, "Garrett, it's about time you started thinking about a place of your own. It's months yet, but not too early to pick out a location and study it."

"Erica said that too. She also said there's a good valley on the other side of that ridge behind Sam's place. Not on the Rim, but good mining and water ice—"

"Yeah. I know the place. Kind of remote. Have to cut a road in. Be even better if we can find a way without cuttin' a road . . ." He muttered to himself for a moment, then said, "Yeah. I like it and the Skipper will like it."

"Okay," I said. "Have I been here long enough to know, or do we go on playing games?"

"How's that?"

"Commander Farr sends you to look me up. You take me in, but we don't mention Farr's name in town. You talk about setting me up on my own, but you like the idea of my going off into the hills without a road. So will Farr. How does it all fit together?"

"Are you sure you want to know?"

I concentrated on driving while I thought about that. "Sarge, I'll do anything you want me to—"

"Didn't ask that. Do you want to know what this is about?"

"Should I?"

"It could be dangerous."

"Is Sam Hendrix in it? Is Erica?"

"Now how can I answer that, Garrett?"

"You've already answered. I think. Sarge, what's Sam Hendrix like? Would he let his daughter marry a convict? Would she care what he said anyway? Would she marry a convict?"

"What do you think?" he asked.

"I think she would. I don't know about him. You told me marriage was pretty serious business on the Rim. And the families get involved deep—"

"They do. Remember what the Skipper told you, Garrett? Nothing counts before you got here. You can be whatever you've got it in you to be. Why the hell should Sam Hendrix care what you did on Earth? You care what he did to get sent here? Or do you think he was a volunteer? Or that Ruth was? You want to marry a convict's daughter, and you ask me if he gives a damn about your background."

"I never thought," I said. I hadn't thought at all. If I had, I'd have guessed that Sam Hendrix had been here forever. And his wife? Ruth Hendrix a transportee? "Whoopeee!"

I startled him. "You gone crazy?" he demanded.

"No. Just happy. Sarge, if you tell me what's going on, will I get her into trouble?"

"Depends on what you do with the information. You don't have to join up, you know. It's a crime to know what we're up to and not report it, but if I don't tell and you don't, who's to know?"

"Okay. You've got a revolution planned. And Commander Farr is in on it."

"Sure," Sarge said. "Hey, the wind's comin' up good. You want me to drive?"

"If you want to—"

"Naw, you're doin' all right. Just watch the downwind sides of the rocks. Sometimes there's holes back there, and they fill up with dust. You can lose the tractor in one if you're not careful. There's no way to protect the Skipper, Garr. He's got to interview recruits and see they don't sign up with some company before we can get to 'em. We've got other inside men, but he's the most exposed."

"Think they suspect him?"

"Nothing to suspect him of. He hasn't done anything yet. Just selected out some transportees for us to put through Marsman training. Like you. Nothin' illegal about that, although you never know what the Feddie bastards will try."

The dust was really blowing thick now, covering the solar cells. The tractor began to lose power. We slowed to a crawl. I glanced at the charge indicator. We were running on direct, not draining the batteries, but we weren't moving very fast.

"Keep with her," Sarge said. "It'll blow off again."

"There's something else bothering me," I said.

"Yeah?"

"You're talking about me going out on my own. That takes a lot. Tractor, airmakers, solar cells, pumps—good Lord, just a lot."

"Yep."

"Damned expensive—"

"Sure is. Don't worry about it, Garrett. We'll swing it. There's more than me on this." He sucked his teeth loudly and smirked at me. "Course, you marry well and you can save me some money. Old Sam's a rich man."

"Sarge!"

"Kids get married and start up on their own, both sets of parents help. Custom out here. Don't turn down a girl because she's rich."

"I wouldn't turn her down if she was a new pilgrim. If she'll have me. But you're not my parent. How do I pay you back?"

"Pay it forward. You'll help two more pilgrims get a start. Nothing big all at once, just over the years you kick in outfits for two. That's the way it works."

"And if I take your stuff and forget it?"

He shrugged. "Your word good?"

"I see." I thought about that all the way back to Windhome.

*　*　*

There were two hundred people packed into Zeke Terman's station, overflowing the main hall and packing the corridors, so many people that I couldn't see how they all got in. And more were coming. It was a Rim gathering.

I had been to one before. That had been a wake. This would be a wedding, but the atmosphere wasn't much different. The Rimrats hold a party to send off an old friend or marry new ones.

Everybody brought what he could: food, beer, wine, whiskey, musical instruments, song collections, or just themselves if things had been rough. We made our own entertainment, and talked treason against the Federation. I didn't know because I didn't have to know, but I suppose three-quarters of those at the gathering were members of the loose organization headed by Commander Alexander Farr. It had no name; it was just a group banded together for Martian independence.

I stood with Erica, not too far from the spot where the ceremony would take place. Henrietta Terman was an old friend of Erica's, and John Appleby had been recruited by one of Sarge's protégés. Appleby stood nervously at the front of the main hall. Then the Padre came in.

At least that's what they called him, and if he had another name, it wasn't used on the Rim. He was vague about which denomination had ordained him back on Earth, and no one knew why he'd been sent to Mars.

The Padre had a station of his own, filled with orphan children and rumored to hold several runaways from company labor contracts. Whenever he was needed the Padre would come, and once a month he made the rounds of the Rim stations whether he was needed or not.

He conducted weddings, spoke words at funerals, held

christenings, and talked treason. He was the Padre, and he had a thousand friends.

Every one of them wanted a word with him. It seemed to take him an hour to get through the press in the Terman main hall, but finally, with John Appleby in tow, he reached his place. Then Zeke Terman brought out his daughter. He held her for a moment, then took her hand and put it into John's and clasped them together. I felt Erica reach for mine.

The Padre read from his leather-bound book for a while. The words were old; I think it was a hundred-year-old *Book of Common Prayer,* and God knows where the Padre got it. Then he closed it and said, "Do you, Henrietta, take this man as your true and only husband, a man to stand by and work with, to have children by and grow old with, and will you remember that he's only a man and forgive him seventy times seven transgressions?"

"I will."

"Who speaks for this man?" the Padre asked.

Harry Bates stood in front of the group. Five years before he had been what I was now, one of Sarge's recruits. Now he had his own station. "I'll stand up with him," Bates said.

"And me too." Sarge had put on his old marine uniform. There was a red stripe down the trousers, and a comet with sunburst on his chest. "I'll stand with him and fight the man who says he's not a Marsman."

"Anybody dispute that?" the Padre asked.

There were a couple of laughs, and somebody shouted, "Nobody crazy here!" That got cheers.

"Okay. Will you, John, take this woman as your true and only wife, and work with her and defend her, build her a home she can be proud to keep for you, and stay away from the whores in town?"

"I will."

The Padre opened his book again. "Okay. There's some more words we need here, but I figure that's mostly what they mean and it don't hurt to put them in plain language." He continued to read, and John and Henrietta gave their responses.

The crowd was fidgety. There was a rumor that John Appleby brewed the best beer on the Rim. Nobody believed it—I certainly didn't, and I still think mine is better

—but we all wanted to sample it. And Terman had set out a splendiferous feed.

Eventually the Padre ran out of words. He closed the book. "In front of Almighty God and these good people, I say you're man and wife. And if any Federation clerk says different, shove it down his throat!"

"YOWEE!" A hundred and more families yelled their approval. Then we headed for the beer.

Later, somehow, they cleared some space for dancing. I don't know where they put the people, because nobody left.

What we call dancing on the Rim isn't exactly what they do on Earth. There are some remnants of Earth square dances in it, but everything is done more violently, with lots of leaping and shouting. In 40 percent gravity that gets spectacular.

There were a lot of girls at the party. I had made up my mind: I was going to meet some of them. I was going to spend time with someone other than Erica so that I'd know it wasn't just the lack of female company in my life that made me feel the way I did whenever she was around.

I meant to, but somehow the evening was over and we hadn't been apart . . .

*　*　*

The main hall in Hellastown was packed: members of nearly every family along Hellas Rim, company representatives, shopkeepers, city dwellers, Federation officials; all were there—and all were talking at once.

There was a guy in natty clothes up on the stage. He kept pounding his gavel for order. His coveralls were a shiny polyester, and they had creases along the trouser legs and sleeves. He didn't wear a p-suit under it. Most of us in the room did, and we smelled, even in thin air. But not him. He was the new administrator for Hellas Region, and he'd never in his life worked hard enough to smell bad.

"Citizens, please!" he shouted. "I cannot listen to your grievances if you all talk at once!"

"Citizens, hell!" I looked over to be sure, and it was Sam Hendrix. "Slaves, that's what you're making us!"

There were plenty of cheers, but they came from the farmers and station owners. The city people were silent. The company reps glared.

"GODDAMN IT, one at a time!" Sarge yelled. He turned toward me and winked. "Let Sam talk for us."

The babble died away. Sam Hendrix got up from his bench and went to the front of the room. He stood on the stairway, but they didn't let him have the microphone. No matter. We could hear him.

"Mister Ellsworth says he has a new charter for us," Sam said. "And the first thing it means is we pay taxes on everything we do! It means ruin—"

"Come now." Administrator Ellsworth didn't have to shout. He simply turned the volume up high so that his amplified voice drowned Sam out. The dapper little creep gave us a big smile. "The charter grants you universal suffrage, and you will have representatives in the General Assembly of Mars. Of course you must pay for these benefits, but how can you object to democracy?"

Sam made a visible effort to control himself. I could see the twitching of the scar on his left cheek. I'd learned that meant he was mad as hell. He did a good job of controlling his voice, though. "Universal suffrage means the labor clients outvote us ten to one. As it is not a secret ballot, they must vote as the companies tell them, or starve. So where does that leave us? We do not require your cities and your Assembly and your rules and your laws. We can take care of ourselves, and we ask only that we be allowed to."

There were more cheers from the Rimrats, but Sam held up his hands for quiet. "Now you are telling us that before we can sell a barrel of beer it must be inspected, and we must pay taxes."

More cheers.

Ellsworth gave Sam a condescending look, the way you might look at a seven-year-old kid who wants to stay up all night to watch the dawn. "Of course we must protect the citizens from harmful products," Ellsworth said. "The new laws will assure wholesome food and drink—"

"We manage that for ourselves," Sam yelled. He was fast losing control. "Don't we?"

"Damn right!" Yeah!" Right on!" "My stuff's good, and

there ain't a man on the Rim don't know it!" All the farmers were shouting.

Sam gestured for quiet again. "Now this Ellsworth gentleman wishes to tax everything we do. Solar cells we make ourselves—"

"We must assure quality." The amplifiers let Ellsworth break in whenever he wanted to. He sounded very smug.

"Even the caves we live in! Building codes he wants to give us! Inspectors in our houses—"

"Your children must be protected. Those stations are not safe," Ellsworth said. His voice took on an edge. "You said you wished to present grievances. These are not grievances, they are no more than bad-mannered complaints. All these measures have the approval of the Federation Council on Earth. Now if you have nothing constructive to say, go home. I have more important things to do than listen to your grumbling. This meeting is adjourned!"

Ellsworth stalked off the stage.

* * *

After that things got worse. They held the elections, but as Sam Hendrix predicted, not a single Rimrat was elected from Hellas Region. They gerrymandered the districts so that we were outvoted by labor clients. "Our" assemblyman was a Mars General corporation lawyer.

We got word from town that some of the miners tried to stand up to Ellsworth and elect one of their own to a seat. Their votes weren't counted, according to rumor; the official word was they were outvoted by "absentee ballots." Sam Hendrix figured that there would have had to be more absentees than registered voters in that district. Ellsworth made sure that nobody else would try that trick: the leaders of the upstart group were sold. Their contracts were transferred to a mining outfit that ran its operation like a slave camp. A couple of them escaped and fled to the Rim, willing to work for shelter and nothing more.

There were now big sales taxes on everything we bought or sold in Hellastown. Federation inspectors forced their way into stations and looked for "structural defects." They turned one family out of a place that had stood safely for fifty years. A big company ended up with title.

Things weren't any better in the other colony areas.

Around Marsport the independent farmers were strong enough to elect two assemblymen, but they were ignored. Katrinkadorp suffered merciless harassment. Mars Taipei was occupied by Federation troops.

Sam Hendrix tried to organize resistance among the Hellas Rimrats. "If we don't sell to the townies, they'll feel it," he said. "Boycott them. Sell no more than it takes to pay for what you have bought. It is better to drive a hundred kilometers to sell to our own people on the Rim than to go ten and sell to Hellastown."

Sarge agreed. We took our produce up into the hills, to mine camps like Inferno where they smelted iron with a big parabolic solar mirror and worked like slaves—but for themselves. We sold to other stations and made do or did without. I set up a solar cell production system; our cells weren't as efficient as those sold in Hellastown, but they worked, and the Rimrats bought them. The boycott was effective.

Even so, Sarge was way down, and I couldn't cheer him up. "I knew it would come to this," he said. We were having our evening drink on the veranda. "Knew it would happen, but goddamn, not so soon. We aren't ready for them yet. Bastards."

He drank down his beer and poured another. "Good stuff. Can sell all we make. That new malting you do is just right. Who needs inspectors? You sell bad beer, nobody buys it. Sell stuff that makes people sick, they'll force a gallon down your throat and laugh like hell. Who needs Hellastown slicks for inspectors?"

"So why are they doing it?" I asked.

Sarge shrugged. "Some of 'em may really think they're protecting us," he said. "Some. But think about it. The big outfits aren't comfortable, having us out here, taking claims they'll want some day. They haven't got the labor to work our claims now, but in twenty years—"

We watched the blowing dust for a while. "About time we had a look at your new claim," Sarge said.

"Yeah." I stared moodily at the electric fire. It wasn't a real fire, of course. It was just an electric heater, but the coils glowed a cheery red.

When I had come to Windhome it had been summer in the southern hemisphere. Now, three-quarters of a Mars year later, it was spring again, and the dust was blowing.

Winter had been hard and cold. We'd cut back to two heated domes, but even for them there wasn't enough solar power to grow many crops. On Mars, winter is a time to stay inside, with a few excursions for Rim gatherings; mostly you dig new tunnels and expand the station. But now, at last, the sun was coming south again.

Halfway across Hellas Basin was the edge of the south polar ice cap, a thin layer of solid carbon dioxide, dry ice, that was now melting off. It's cold out there in winter, but not as cold as you might think—that is, the temperature is low enough to freeze the carbon dioxide out of the air, but the air is so thin that it doesn't conduct heat away very fast. If you've got properly insulated clothing, you can get around, even at night if you're careful to insulate yourself from the ground. You've also got to watch radiation—wear dark outer covering in the daytime to pick up heat, and light colored at night to avoid throwing heat to space.

Now the dust was blowing. Winter was nearly over. It was time. I liked the idea of getting out on my own, and I was pretty sure how Erica would answer when I asked her to marry me and help set up the new station. But Sarge was my friend, the best friend I'd ever had. It was sad to think of leaving.

He must have guessed what I was thinking. "Skipper's got a new crop comin' in, and we've got to move fast now. Things are comin' apart. Skipper wants us to cycle three recruits at each of our stations. About the time I get three broke in, maybe you'll need help with your new place and I can palm one off on you."

"I see. Sink or swim time."

"You'll be outfitted pretty good," Sarge said. "Between what I can give you, and what Sam will put up."

"If she says yes."

"She will. I notice you've been to four Rim gatherin's now, and she puts in all her time with you. Other guys don't even ask her anymore. You'd better marry her, you've cut her off from the other suitors—"

"I wish I could be as sure of that as you are," I said. But I was, really. "If you're so damned anxious to have people married, why aren't you?"

His grin faded. "Was, Garr. She's dead. Maybe I'd like to try it again, but now's the wrong time. Hey, I bought some more germanium from Sam. Closed the deal on the radio this afternoon. Tomorrow you can go pick it up for me."

"Sure. Thanks."

He nodded, but he was staring out at the dust storm. He hadn't liked the news he was hearing from town.

I was interested in politics, sure, but just then I was a lot more interested in getting over to Ice Hill.

8

By now I had the status of a regular guest—not that hospitality wouldn't have been splendid for any Rim visitor. By custom, any traveler was welcome at any station—but in my case I got a complete discourse on politics from Sam whenever I showed up.

When he invited me into his study after lunch, I figured it was politics time again, but he surprised me. He used the intercom to send for his wife, and he asked Erica to come in as well. While we were waiting for Ruth, he poured a drink for all of us.

Ruth Hendrix was smiling as she came in.

Sam rather formally invited us to sit down. I was beginning to wonder what was happening, but Erica was grinning, so I wasn't worried.

"Well," Sam said. "Sarge tells me that you are about to go choose a location for your own station."

I nodded. I'd never seen Sam so slow at getting to the point.

"He has also told me that he wishes to speak to me about something rather important. As your sponsor, Garrett."

"Oho."

"I beg your pardon?"

"Yes, sir. He's pushing things a little, but—"

"Not pushing them at all. Now, I have had business dealings with Sarge Wechsung before. This is likely to cost me at least one arm and probably both legs. Before I go to that trouble, has anyone here an objection?"

Ye gods, I thought. I looked at Erica. She was shaking with repressed laughter, but trying to hide it from her father. Sam was trying not to notice.

"I think it's a splendid idea," Ruth Hendrix said. "And I know Erica does. Don't you, Ricky?"

Well, we got through it somehow. Nobody objected. We weren't engaged, not exactly, and wouldn't be until the negotiations between Sarge and Sam were finished and it was all announced; but as far as Erica and I were concerned, we were going to be married. Sam and Ruth even found an excuse to leave us alone for a few minutes.

The whole thing makes more sense than it probably seems to. On the Rim you can't just go off and set up housekeeping. Once in a while a Rim girl marries a town man, usually without her folks' approval, and if he's got a job she can move into town and that's that; but to open a new station requires a lot of equipment, and a lot more work than two people can do in a short time.

The parents have to help. If they've got to put up all that money, they're going to have a say in who gets it. And a new couple won't be independent, not really, for several years anyway, and if they can't make a go of it— not necessarily through their own fault, things can go wrong here despite all you can do—they've got to have a place to go.

So it makes sense that the parents have to approve, and there's no point in the prospective couple getting too involved unless that approval is likely, and there's no point in all the negotiations and purchases and arrangements unless the couple approve of each other; thus the complicated formalities.

We didn't care, of course. I wasn't thinking about how it made sense. I was too damned happy to think about anything.

When Sam came back into his study he purposely made a lot of noise. "Sorry to break things up," he said. "But Garrett will have to be going. I do not like to see you travel without plenty of daylight. The dust is very thick today."

He was right. I looked around for my hat. We'd already loaded the germanium into Aunt Ellen.

"Erica, I believe you wanted to go into town," Sam said. "And there are errands you can do for me, as well. I no longer care to go there unless I must."

"Sure," she said.

"Excellent. I suggest you go to Windhome with Garrett, and take the agricultural co-op tractor into Hellastown in the morning. It comes by your place tomorrow, does it not?"

I had to think. Ellsworth had decreed that the co-op could only sell in Hellastown. We didn't have much business for the co-op anymore. "Yes, sir."

"You will have to bring her back when she returns, but I doubt you will mind that."

Erica went to get her travel kit. It looked like this would be a splendid day, even if the dust was blowing up a bit thick.

We had a short delay after we were out of sight of Sam's place, but I didn't want to waste too much daylight. The dust was indeed thick, and although we had plenty of time, Sam was right: the more daylight you have ahead of you, the better off you are. Tractors do break down, and although Aunt Ellen never had, there was always a first time.

We talked about our new place, and laughed at the way Sam had acted, and wondered what we'd feel like when we had a daughter who wanted to get married. We babbled about the Project, and about Earth, and about how many kids we wanted, and what kind of floor plan we wanted when we started blasting out our home, and an hour and a half went by very quickly. Then I heard the voice on the radio. We had come into line-of-sight with Windhome, although we couldn't see it because of the dust.

"Garrett, this is Sarge. Do not answer. Garrett, Garrett, Garrett, this is Sarge. Do not answer."

"What the hell?" I said.

"Garrett, this is Sarge. Do not answer. Stop and listen carefully. Do not answer."

"There's something terribly wrong," Erica said.

"Garrett, if you can hear me, do exactly what I say. Punch the fourth channel button from the left, fourth from the left. Turn on the set and say you can hear. Say nothing else and turn it off quick. Keep the transmission as short as possible. Okay, if you hear me, go. Over."

I hit the button and lifted the mike. "Sarge, I hear you. Over."

"Thank God, I've been calling for an hour. Garrett, Ellsworth sent the cops after me. They're trying to break the boycott. I'm holed up, but they've got me located. They may be listening to this. They'll have me in a minute. Don't come back here, they'll put you in the bucket. Look up our friends, and warn the Rim. They knocked out the photophone and our main antenna, so all I've got left is short-range. Warn 'em along the Rim. Do not answer me, they'll locate you if you do."

"We've got to do something," I said.

Erica nodded. "Yes. The first thing is to alert the Rim. Sarge is right, we've got to get the word out."

Sarge's voice came through again. "Sorry it worked out this way, kid. I wanted to set you up better, but it looks like I won't be doing that. You've got other friends, though. They'll help. You're a good man, Garrett. Here they come."

There were loud sounds like explosions, then a whistling wind. "Blowout!" I said. I looked at Erica. She nodded. It had to be a blowout, and Sarge was in it.

"They've smashed their way in," she said.

"We've got to do something. I've got to see what's happening—"

"All right," she said. "But the first thing is to hide this tractor. If we drive up there, they'll have us too."

I thought about that. "Right. We can walk from here. It's not too far." I took Aunt Ellen off the road and out into the boulder fields. We found a hollow full of dust. I drove into it, and the wind whipped more dust around us. Pretty soon the tractor would be hidden. The tracks leading in from the road were already covered over.

I switched on the pumps. By the time we had put our helmets on the air from the cabin was stored in tanks.

"We won't be able to use the suit radios," Erica warned. "They'll hear us."

"Yeah." We got out, and I looked around carefully. It wouldn't do to hide the tractor so well we couldn't find it again. There was a big split rock about ten meters away, and I looked up at the stars to get a bearing from it to the tractor. We had about three hours of daylight left, maybe a little more, but not much. When night came we'd have to be inside, either in a tractor or in a shelter.

When we were sure we could find Aunt Ellen again, we started walking for Windhome. Erica was young and healthy, but she had trouble keeping up with me. That's one advantage to being born on Earth. I was used to weighing over twice as much as I did on Mars, and even with all the air tanks and other gear it wasn't hard going. I wished we had weapons, but we didn't, except for our knives and some tools in our belt kits.

I led her up the side of the Chamberpot, a tattered rimwall that stands next to Windhome. Sarge called it the Devil's Pisspot, but the official mapmakers wouldn't use that. The Chamberpot's rim has cracks that lead to Windhome, and I was sure nobody knew about them.

It was tricky climbing the side of the hill, and if you run too hard, you use a lot of air. We scrambled up the steep sides of the crater to the top, then down into the bowl. There was a ledge just inside the rim. It dropped off sheer for a hundred meters on our right, and it wasn't very wide. Until I watched her two-step along a section not much wider than my foot, I worried about Erica. Then I worried about myself.

I couldn't talk to her because the cops might be listening. I wondered if they'd heard Sarge's message to me. If they had they'd be looking for us, but they wouldn't know in what direction I'd been coming. There's a lot of desolate area around Windhome. I decided we were safe for the moment.

At the end of the ledge there was a crack through the rimwall. It was just wide enough to get through. Once inside it we were in deep shadow, but even through the dust we could see stars out above us like night. Then we were looking down on Windhome.

The station was in ruins. All the domes were cracked open, and the air-lock doors had been blown off their hinges.

There were more explosions as we stood watching. We

couldn't hear them, of course, but we could see dust blow out of openings, and one of the tunnels collapsed. I stood in a boiling rage, trying to decide what to do. Mostly I wanted to kill people. A lot of them.

A group filed out of the main entrance. I had brought the binoculars from the tractor, and I could see them clearly: Federation Marines, carrying rifles. Seven of them had slugthrowers, and another had a big powerpack and laser rifle. After a short interval two more came out. One of them was Sarge. I could tell from his walk. They had him in handcuffs, but he was alive!

I grabbed Erica and pointed. She nodded. Then she held up her belt radio and pointed to the frequency dial. It took me a moment to catch on—I thought she wanted to talk, which was stupid of me. She knew better. When I tuned the receiver to the frequency she showed me, I heard voices.

"Where is he, Wechsung?"

"Go to hell."

"Look, we know your tractor is missing. Where did he go?"

"Get dorked."

One of the men hit Sarge with his rifle butt. I heard Sarge grunt, then he said, "Bielenson, you were a slimy bastard when I was in the service. You haven't changed."

"Maybe not. Take a good look, Wechsung. You men, get a lot of photos of this place. We'll show these farmers what happens to rebels. They'll straighten up."

I put my helmet against Erica's. When they touched we could talk without radios. "We've got to do something!"

"Hold on, my muscular friend," she said. "What will happen if you go charging down there?"

"Yeah." They had rifles and we had knives. There were at least ten of them, probably more in their tractors, and two of us. Three if we counted Sarge, but he was handcuffed.

"Gary, I know how you feel, but the best thing we can do is get back and tell Dad. And you've got your orders, mister. Sarge told you to alert the Rim."

She was right, but I didn't like it. I stood there trembling with helpless rage. They started boarding the three tractors. Two of them pushed Sarge into the small one and got in after him. "We could follow them," I said.

"On foot? Don't be an idiot."

"Varadd. Rogers," the radio said. "Get inside and stay out of sight. When that kid shows up, grab him."

"Sir. How long will we be here, major?"

"I'm leaving you air for two days. We'll be back for you before sundown tomorrow. Just now we've got other work to do."

"Sir." The marine sounded unhappy about being left there.

"Load up and move out."

There was a babble of voices, and the rest of them got into the tractors. They started up, the two big tractors turning eastward toward Hendrix station. The small one with Sarge and two marines turned west onto the Hellastown road.

"Come on," Erica said. She pulled away from me and ran back through the crack. For a moment I didn't move. I wanted to see what happened to Sarge, but she was right; we couldn't follow tractors on foot. By running away from me she kept me from doing something stupid. I ran after her.

We dashed along the ledge inside Pisspot's Rim. She was much faster than I on that narrow ledge, and she got a long way ahead. Then she was over the top. I caught up to her on the way down. Going down was easy—a twenty-foot drop was nothing. I had to be careful, though, because for the same speed you've got the same momentum on Mars as on Earth, you just weigh less. Still, I took that slope like it was a giant staircase. There was dust on the road below, and the faint marks of tractors.

We crossed the road and ran to Aunt Ellen. When we got inside, I brought the pressure up so we could talk.

"They're going to Ice Hill," she said. "They'll arrest my father! And Mom, too, maybe everyone there—"

"If they mean to blow up Ice Hill the way they did Windhome, they'll have to take everybody."

"We've got to warn them!"

"Yeah." I thought about the tracks I'd seen on the road. "But we've only got line-of-sight communications and they're ahead of us on the road. Just how do we warn them?"

9

Erica looked at the map, then pointed. "Take us out into the Basin. Right there."

She pointed at a rise about a kilometer from where we'd hidden Aunt Ellen. It was straight away from the Rim, not in the direction either of the Federation groups had gone. I thought of the tractor with Sarge in it getting away toward Hellastown, and the other two approaching Ice Hill. "Why?"

"Just do it. I'll tell you on the way."

"All right." I started the tractor and began picking a way through the boulder fields. There was no road or track. The map had been made by satellite photograph; I doubt that any human had ever been this way before. "Okay, why?"

"Because it will be in line of sight to Ice Hill. I think. It looks high enough."

"Dust is pretty thick—"

"If we can't get through with the photophone we'll use the radio."

"All right." I tried for more speed, but there were pits and rocks everywhere, and the dust made it hard to see. When summer comes, the dry ice on one polar cap boils off rather than melting—and blows all the way to the opposite pole. That raises big winds in Hellas. "One good thing," I said. "There's so much dust that they'll never see us out here. We can't be stirring up enough more to matter."

It took a good half hour to make that one kilometer. The hill she'd indicated was a mound about 250 meters high, a big bubble that had formed when Hellas was a lava field a billion years ago. When we reached the top, we were above a lot of the dust storm. I turned the telescope onto the Rim east of us, and searched for Ice Hill.

"There it is," I said. "I can just make out the photophone target."

Not all tractors have talking-light units, but Sarge kept Aunt Ellen better equipped than most Rimrats can afford. The sight was built into our telescope. I trained it onto the white photophone target at the top of Ice Hill, then used the joystick to get a precise adjustment. The system uses a modulated laser beam and has to be aimed just right. The advantage is that nobody can listen in unless they're in the exact line of sight, and you can see along that.

"Ice Hill, Ice Hill, Ice Hill. Mayday. Answer by photophone only. We are on Hill 252, Basin Sector Greeneight. Mayday." Erica said that several times. We waited.

"Sis! That you? I can hardly hear you."

"Perry, get Dad. Quickly."

"What's that?"

"I said get Dad. *Now!*"

There was a long delay. "The dust is interfering with the beam," Erica said.

"Just be damn glad we can get through at all."

"I am. Have I told you I love you?"

"Not often enough."

"Erica, what is happening? Why have you two left the road? What are you doing in the Basin?"

"Dad, listen!" She managed to cut him off. If we'd been using radio and had to wait for him to say "over" and switch from transmit to receive, we might be there yet.

She told him what had happened at Windhome. "And two tractors full of Federation Marines, with that officer, Bielenson, left Windhome toward Ice Hill an hour ago," she finished.

"So you think they are coming for me?"

"I don't know," I said. "But they blew up Windhome and arrested Sarge."

"It is possible. It even makes sense," Sam said. "With Sarge and myself arrested and our stations ruined as an example to others, the boycott might well collapse. Yes, I think that is what they have in mind. But it is very late in the day. There is barely enough sunlight for them to reach us in time. Perhaps they will wait until morning—"

"Dad, you've got to get away!" Erica said.

"Get away? Run? No, Ricky. If they come to destroy my home, they must take it from me."

I didn't know it then, but that very second marked the beginning of the Martian War of Independence.

*　*　*

We cut off so that Sam could organize his family to fight. As with Windhome there was no way we could help. We couldn't get there; we had barely enough sunlight to get to the road.

"At least you're safe," I said. "Now what can we do? Try to follow the tractor they put Sarge in? They'll have a long start."

"Yes." She wasn't really listening to me. She was looking out at the Rim to the west.

"I suppose we'd better find a good place out of the wind. We'll be out here for the night—"

"Garrett! That's Zeke Terman's station up there!"

"Yeah. And he can see the road. At least we can find out what the cops are doing." I slewed Aunt Ellen around and aimed the telescope. It was much easier this time; we were a lot closer to Zeke's place than we were to Ice Hill.

Erica lifted the mike and went through the calling routine: "Zeke Terman, Zeke Terman, Zeke Terman, Mayday, Mayday, Mayday. Answer by photophone only. We are on Hill 252, Sector Green-eight. Mayday." She repeated it three times. We had to give our location, because the transmitting laser must be aimed at the receiver.

Finally we got an answer. "Mayday, this is Terman. What the hell are you doing out there? Who are you?"

"You'll recognize my voice," Erica said. "Are you alone? Are you all right?"

"Why the hell shouldn't I be all right? Of course I'm alone, think I've got crew to take off work and chat on the goddamn phone?"

"Zeke, this is an emergency. Please answer a silly question. It's important that we can be sure you're alone and all right. What does Henrietta call her cat?"

There was a moment of silence. Then Zeke said, "Ricky Hendrix? That you? Henrietta calls the silly animal 'Titwillow' because of something you said. What's going on?"

We told him.

"Son of a bitch! Okay, I'll relay the word down the west Rim. Where did they take Sarge?"

"They put him in a tractor and headed west on the Hellastown road about an hour ago," Erica said.

"Wait one," Zeke told us. He left the mike open, and we heard him shouting. "Bonnie, get the boys up here! Get everybody. Come running!" Then there was silence for a while, and he came back on the line. "Okay, I've got the tractor spotted, I think. Bright yellow?"

"Right!"

"Not makin' very good time with all this dust. They're still a good half hour from Iron Gap. I'll get the boys and be to the Gap before the cops get there. A couple of sticks of 40 percent and they'll not be getting to Hellastown tonight."

"By God!" I said. "We can get Sarge loose!" I took the mike from Erica. "Thanks, Zeke."

"That you, Garrett? Thanks, hell. That's my son-in-law's sponsor those bastards have in that tractor. You want in this fight, you'd better hurry to the Gap!"

* * *

Mars is at the inner edge of the asteroid belt, and has very little atmosphere. When a big chunk of rock hits, as frequently happens—frequent meaning every hundred thousand years or so—the impact raises ringwall craters that stay until another rock breaks them down, or the wind slowly grinds them into dust. There's no rain to erode the mountains.

The crater that became the Wall was formed by a meteriod a billion years ago. Countless other rocks smashed into the old ringwall, until only one stretch was left, and that was cracked down the center. This cracked wall lies directly across the road from the eastern Rim stations to Hellastown. The crack is called Iron Gap, and it's no more than twenty feet wide in some places. You don't *have* to go through the Gap to get to Hellastown, but the quickest way around takes five hours of travel through the boulder fields, or even longer if you try to climb the Wall with a tractor.

I looked at it on the map but didn't start the tractor.

"What are you waiting for?" Erica demanded.

"Your father will kill me if I take you into a battle."

"You let me worry about my father. Do you think I'm fragile? That I can't take care of myself? I may not be as strong as you are, but you're not going to leave me out of this!"

"All right, all right. I'm sorry. But I've got about a million years of instincts that say I shouldn't do this." I started the tractor, and headed toward the Gap.

"Instincts be damned. Mars is more my home than yours! Oh, I'm sorry, Gary. I don't really mean that. We both live here."

"You don't have to be sorry. I was never very interested in the independence movement. I'm not now. But Sarge is my friend, and the Feddies won't let us get out here and live, they've got to mess everything up. And ruin the only home I've ever been happy in—"

I couldn't finish. Thinking about Windhome as I'd last seen it brought tears, and I needed to see as well as I could to get through the boulders and dust.

After we reached it, I decided to chance the road. Daylight would be gone in less than an hour, and we'd never reach the Gap across country. I'd never had Aunt Ellen going this fast before.

"Reckless Garrett, The Terror of the Martian Roadways," I said. "Whoopee!"

"You like this, don't you?" She was very serious.

"Like it? My home's in ruins, my buddy's been taken by the cops, we may both be killed, and—"

"And you love it. It's all right, Gary. But you do. You want to fight. I think all men do. I wonder if women ever feel that way? I never did. Is it something instinctual, or do you learn it, or—"

"Good Lord, girl!"

"I'm sorry. I'm scared, that's all. No, don't slow down, I'm going with you. And I love you."

"I didn't start this fight."

"No. Some men learn to control that love of combat. But you're not sorry it has started. You'll cry for Windhome, and for friends who are killed, and you'll be glad when it's over, but you're not sorry it started."

"You're a nut."

"Sure."

We rounded a curve, and suddenly the Gap was in sight, about ten kilometers ahead. I drove on. Then, 250 meters above the Gap floor, there was a startling spurt of dust from one of the straight-walled sides. Something big dislodged and fell into the Gap, sealing it.

"They'll not get through there before sunset," I said. "They must not have reached the Gap yet! Zeke wouldn't do that if they were already through!"

"I wonder how far ahead they are?"

"Don't know, but I'm not going to stop to talk," I said. The sun was almost to the Rim ahead of us. Soon we'd be in shadow, and after that we'd be on battery power.

Erica began fiddling with the radio. She didn't turn on the transmitter, but swept through all the bands, listening—

"Four Love Victor, this is One Dog Niner. Four Love Victor, this is One Dog Niner. Mayday. Mayday. Over."

"The cops," Erica said.

They went on calling.

"They can't raise Hellastown. They're in the shadow of the Wall!" I said. "They're on battery power, and out of line of sight to anywhere! The cops are cut off."

We'd run out of sun pretty soon, too. "Okay," I said. "Try to raise Zeke. I don't care if the cops hear us now. What can they do?"

"Right."

"Just a minute, Hon. Listen!"

The cop was still calling. There was a plaintive note in his voice. Then I heard it again: a big booming laugh.

"Shut up Wechsung or we'll shut you up!" the cop said.

"Sure." Sarge's voice was faint, too far from the mike to hear distinctly. "You boys are in big trouble. Maybe you better let me talk to my buddies out there before they roll rocks on top of this thing."

"Shut up, Wechsung. Four Love Victor, Mayday. Mayday!"

* * *

It was pitch dark before Zeke guided us to where he and his sons had stationed themselves. He had two tractors, a big pressurized trailer with a portable powerpack, and oxygen-hydrogen fuel cells in another trailer. The police would have to rely on their internal batteries, but we had power to burn. We hooked Aunt Ellen into Zeke's system and went into his trailer.

Zeke was there with one of his sons, Ezra. John Appleby was there as well. They had a coffee pot going, and food.

"Cops have been callin' us," Zeke said. "I think they're scared. They keep tellin' us how Sarge doesn't have a helmet on. We haven't answered 'em yet."

"Think they'd let Sarge loose if we promise to leave 'em alone?" I asked.

Zeke shrugged. "Could be. Garrett, I haven't talked to 'em yet, because they don't know I'm in this. Might be a good idea not to tell 'em. Anyway, I thought I'd wait for you and Johnny here. You two got the biggest stake in this game—"

"They already want me," I said. "May as well let me do the talking. John has a pregnant wife. No point in getting you involved, John."

"Yeah, but—"

"If you have to be, you will be," Zeke said. "I was hoping you'd say something like that, Garrett. I blew out the road, and I'll go in after the bastards if that's what it takes. But I don't mind sayin' I'd as soon not see my station blown up the way Windhome was."

"What are we up against?" I asked.

John Appleby answered. "I've seen it. The tractor's no tank, but they've got a machine-gun turret mounted on top, and they've got thick plate on it. We could take it, no question about it. They've moved off into a clear space—they're going to be damned cold by morning if they stay out in the wind—so we can't drop rocks on their heads, but we could probably get close enough to throw dynamite. But I don't see any way we can get inside that thing without killing Sarge."

"Expect reinforcements?" I asked.

Zeke shrugged. "Don't think they got a message through. Hellastown isn't going to be anxious to send out a force in the dark. Never get tanks through the Gap anyway, they'd have to go around, and they won't do *that* at night. My other boy's watchin' from up on the side of the Gap, and he'll tell us if he sees lights comin', but I think we've got till morning for sure."

"Yeah. Well, let's talk to them. Worse comes to worse, we'll offer a trade." I drank the coffee Zeke had given me, then went over and sat down in front of the radio. The trailer was big and cozy. Zeke used it as a mobile prospecting camp.

"One Dog Niner, are you listening? Over."

"Yeah, we're listening. You bastards better let us go! There'll be two battalions of marines with tanks out here by morning!"

"This won't last until morning," I said. "You've got troubles, fellows. Now let me hear Sarge talking."

"Why?"

"Because any time I ask to hear him and I don't, I'm going to assume he's dead, and there won't be any reason why we shouldn't be throwing dynamite. Clear? We've got more power than you have. You can't run away from us, so don't waste batteries. Just put Sarge on."

There was a pause. Then, "Hey kid. You're doin' okay."

"You all right, Sarge?"

"Sure. Look, don't let 'em talk you into nothing, they're—"

"That's enough," the policeman said. "He's all right."

"Good. You keep him that way. I'll be back in a bit. Out." I switched off the transmitter.

"The trouble is," I said, "they think they can wait for sunlight and just take off. With that machine gun they know they can put any tractor we've got out of action. And there probably will be reinforcements before noon. We need a way to convince them we can disable them without hurting Sarge—"

We thought for a moment. Then I had an idea. "John,

you said you can hit them with dynamite. Can you hit them with paint?"

"Paint?"

"Yeah. In a plastic bag. If we splatter paint on their windscreen and solar cells, where are they going in the morning?"

"Be damned," Zeke said. "Ezra, get on the photophone and tell your mother we need some paint down here. Paint and some bags." He turned back to me. "She won't like that. Damn bags are expensive and we can't make 'em."

"It's for a good cause. Maybe we won't need many."

"I'll throw," John said. "If I can't talk, I ought to be of some use."

It took half an hour to organize, and I let the cops stew for another half hour. We were in no real hurry. By now it would be getting cold in their tractor, even with the heaters going. Then John moved into position.

"Okay, ready," he said.

We had two radios, so we could keep John on one and use the other to talk to the cops. I called them.

"Yeah?"

"Let me hear Sarge."

"Still okay, kid."

"Good," I said. "Now. What's your name, whichever of you is in charge?"

"What's that to you?"

"I don't really care, but I ought to call you some-thing—"

"Call him Stinky," Sarge said in the background.

"Shut up, Wechsung. My name is Larkin."

"All right, Larkin, watch close now." I switched to the other radio. "Let her fly!"

There was nothing for a moment. Then John's voice came through. "Right on target! Hit the windscreen."

"Beautiful." I called Larkin again. "Get the message? How far will you get in the morning with the solar panels covered with black paint? Oh, and don't try moving the tractor. You'll waste power you're going to need be-fore the night's over, and there's no place you can go that we can't get upwind of you."

"He's shooting hell out of the rocks," John reported. "I wonder what he thinks he can hit?"

"Can you whap him again?"

"Sure. Here goes."

I called again. "Well, Larkin? How much air have you got? Think your relief can get through the Gap before you run out? Ready to give up, or should we paint the whole tractor for you?"

"Damn you! It's Pittson, isn't it? You're in trouble, Pittson. Let us go and we can straighten it out. Nobody's been hurt yet—"

I laughed at him.

He was off for five minutes. We waited. Then he came on. "Okay. You win. We'll turn Wechsung loose in the morning, if you hold off the paint until then—"

"Crap. You're no Marsman. Our word's good. Yours isn't," I said.

"Attaboy!" Sarge shouted in the background.

"Shut up, Wechsung. Pittson, if we let him go, will you leave us alone? Nobody around in the morning?"

"What about it, Sarge?" I asked.

"Take 'em up on it."

"Roger."

Appleby brought Sarge into the trailer a few minutes later. We got his helmet off. "You okay?" I asked.

"Few bruises. Nothing to worry about. Damn good to have friends. Thanks."

"Sure."

"Sandwiches and coffee here," Zeke said.

"Thanks." Sarge wolfed a sandwich and washed it down with black coffee. "But we got more troubles. Erica, did you kids get through to Sam? I think they went after him—"

"Yes," she said. She told him what we'd done. "Dad said he'd fight. I'm worried—"

"He'll be all right for now," Sarge said. "By now he'll have plenty of friends there. Okay, Sam's taken care of. Zeke, can you get through to Chris Martin's place?" Martin's station was on the other side of the Gap, toward Hellastown from us.

"Sure. Want me to patch you in from here?"

"Please. And get some night traveling gear together. I have to walk across the Gap tonight."

"Tonight?" Erica demanded. "Why?"

"Only way to connect with Chris and get a tractor to Hellastown," Sarge said. "They've got the Skipper in the jug, and I've got to get him out. I could use some help. Any volunteers?"

He was looking directly at me.

10

"It's not as crazy as it sounds," Sarge said. "We always knew the Skipper would be the first one arrested when the Feddies made their move, so we took some precautions. And they don't know we're coming. They still think everything's all right out here. Last report Ellsworth heard I was in custody, Windhome was a wreck, and they were off to Ice Hill, moving on Sam at first light tomorrow, and him not knowing a thing about it. This is the right time for it."

"Well, long as it's going to be a piece of cake, I'll come along," John Appleby said.

What could I do? "Me too."

"Only need one," Sarge said. "Rather have Garrett. No offense, Johnny, but they already want him." He didn't add that Appleby already had a going station and so was less expendable than me. He didn't have to.

Zeke brought in extra clothing. Sarge used the set to call Chris Martin and arrange for him to meet us on the other side of the Gap. Martin was an old grad, one of Commander Farr's first recruits. He'd come to Mars with his whole family, and now his children were out on their own.

I asked John to take Erica to Ice Hill in the morning.

The battle would be over before they could get there. "If things aren't right," I said, "let the Padre know where you've taken her—"

"Sure. Everything'll be okay. What with Sam's family and the friends he'll have coming, those Feddies won't know what hit 'em."

Sarge finished his radio call. "Won't take him long, he's got an auxilliary power trailer for night work. Garr, you about ready?"

"Just about." I felt like an Eskimo: p-suit, reflective coveralls, foam-insulated jacket and pants, another jacket, and more coveralls over the whole mess. I looked like a cartoon. I tried to hug Erica, and it was comical; with all the clothes I had on I could hardly feel her against me.

"Please come back—" She reached up through my open face plate and stroked my cheek. We could just touch lips through the face opening of my helmet.

"I'll be back."

It was cold out. The wind was up to 150 kilometers an hour, a hurricane on Earth. I'd been wrong about Martian winds. The air's too thin for the wind to have much force. It put no more pressure on us than a ten-mile-an-hour wind on Earth, but it was cold. I could feel it through all my clothes.

We didn't have far to go. Around the police tractor, then through the Gap. Zeke had blocked it good: there were three boulders the size of houses, and a lot of smaller rubble. We had to climb over.

We didn't dare show a light. Sarge didn't trust the cops. "Not that Larkin's such a bad sort," he said. "But he's scared. If he sees lights he may figure we're going to do him in no matter what you promised. Best not to take chances."

When we were through the Gap we had more light. Phobos was rising on the other side. The little moon moves so fast that it goes from west to east. I stumbled a few times, but we only had to walk about half a kilometer. The tractor wasn't there yet, and we walked on down the road. It was too cold to stand still.

Then we saw the lights, and the tractor drove up. We got in, and Sarge introduced me to Chris. He was a short, dark man who didn't talk much. There was nobody with him.

It had been a long day, and we had more to do before it was over. The motors hummed as we raced through the night. I figured Sarge would tell me when it was time, and there wasn't much to talk about. I crawled into the bunk behind the seat and tried to sleep.

* * *

"Okay, kid, we're here."

"I wasn't asleep, Sarge." I moved so I could see out the windscreen. There was a big man-made cylinder topped by a dome about a kilometer away. It looked enormous.

"Observatory," Sarge said. "Don't figure they'll be guarding it yet. It's run by some big-name scientists from all the best universities, and Ellsworth won't want the kind of trouble they can make for him if he gets in their way."

"I never knew there was an observatory," I said.

"Yep. And it's not all that far from the school. Larkin was joking about how they had the Skipper locked up in his own cells. Thought that was funny."

"As funny as bubble gum in a lockjaw ward, as the saying goes. Now what, Sarge?"

"Now Chris stays with the tractor—"

"I could—"

"Chris, I don't need heroes! If two can't get Mr. Farr out, three can't either, and I may want you to move this heap in a hurry. You know tractors better than Garr, so you stay."

"All right."

"That's settled, then. Garr, we'll climb into the observatory. The scientists won't be looking for us, and if anyone does see us, act like you belong there. They come from so many different places they can't all know each other, and they've got no reason to be suspicious if we don't get in their way."

"Right." I was getting the shakes, but I wasn't going to show it. I began zipping and velcro-ing myself into all my layers of clothing.

Phobos was higher now, so it wasn't quite as dark as it had been in the Gap. The little moon gave enough light to help us pick our way across the badlands. The observatory was on a high peak behind Hellastown where there wasn't any blowing dust; they'd picked the location because there was seldom any wind in this spot.

Sarge had a length of nylon line with a hook on the end made from a bent jack handle. He threw the hook upward into the dark. It fell back soundlessly, and he threw it again. This time it caught. He tugged on the line, then put his weight on it and swung back and forth. Then he pressed his helmet against mine.

"I'll go first. Come up when I give three tugs. No need to put both our weights on this thing."

"Rog."

He climbed upward and in seconds was only a dark shape against the stars. I waited for what seemed like hours. I'd worked up a sweat coming up the hill, and now, despite the still air, I felt the cold and began to shiver. Then the rope jerked three times. I began climbing.

It was easy. Despite all the gear, I weighed a lot less than I would on Earth. I pulled myself up, hand over hand, until I reached an open ironwork balcony that ran around the outside of the observatory. Sarge gave me a hand over the rail. Then he led the way around until we came to the big telescope opening, and we could look down inside.

Four or five people, bundled up the way we were, moved purposefully on the floor below. They didn't look up at all. The telescope was directly in front of us, looking as if it were staring at us, but of course it was peering at something billions of miles away. A silly thought popped into my head: what would happen if I stood on the rail and made faces into the tube?

There was another walkway around the inside of the dome, and we stepped through onto that, then climbed down an iron ladder to the floor below. One of the people down there glanced up at us, then went back to work. He may have reserved all his curiosity for the universe; I can't imagine what he thought we were doing up there. On the other hand, I haven't any idea of what he was doing either.

No one paid any attention to us as we went across to the air-lock entrance and cycled through. The corridor beyond was empty. When we'd dogged shut the door, we opened our faceplates. "Piece of cake," Sarge said.

"So far."

"Yeah. Watch for cops." He led the way along the corridor, then down another. It was steep downhill all the way. Eventually we came to a steel door set in the corridor wall. Sarge used a key to open it, showing a closet filled with janitor's gear.

"Told you we'd made a few preparations. Skipper was supposed to come out this way." Sarge did something to the shelving and the whole closet swung out on hinges. We went through, closing both doors behind us.

We had to use helmet lights in the narrow, dark passage. It went steeply downward, bending at right angles a couple of times. "Hard rock," Sarge said. "Easier to drill around than through. Here, hold on."

He stopped at a stretch of corridor wall that looked like all the rest, and examined it until he found a tiny hole. He took off a glove, reached in, and pulled with his finger. A coverplate came out revealing a cavity behind it.

"Know anything about guns?" he asked.

"I've shot them. I'm no expert."

"Yeah. Well, here." He handed me a police revolver. "There aren't a lot of guns on Mars. Keep that hid good, anybody sees you with it, they'll *know* you don't belong here." He pocketed another pistol, and a grenade. "Not much for weapons, but better'n just knives. Okay, be kind of quiet from here on. This ends up behind the shelves in the Old Man's office. There may be somebody there. If there is, we have to jump him before he can call. But we want him alive—"

"Rog."

"Piece of cake," Sarge said. He grinned. "Let's do it."

There was a peephole at the end of the passage. Sarge peered through it, then motioned to me.

The door was closed, and a man sat at the desk. I nodded, and Sarge opened the panel.

It was simple. Sarge had him by the throat while I got his hands so he couldn't touch any of the console buttons. We held him like that.

"Easy, now," Sarge said. "One peep, and you're dead."

He got a knife out of his belt and held it at our prisoner's throat. "You understand that?"

He nodded.

"It's Hardesty," I said. "He was our barracks sergeant."

Sarge let him go, but held the knife in place. Hardesty gulped hard. I got his hands behind the chair and took a couple of turns of line around them. Then we wheeled him away from the desk so he couldn't reach anything.

"Where's Mr. Farr?" Sarge demanded.

"Interrogation room," Hardesty said. He was careful not to speak above a whisper. "Mr. Ellsworth was in there for a while, but he went back over to town."

"You night duty NCO?"

"Yes."

"Okay. Now I'm going to have you use that intercom to send for Mr. Farr. Before I do, I want to tell you what happens to you if you try anything funny." Sarge hitched the knife in his hand, tossing it wickedly up and down. "I won't kill you. But you'll father no more kids, and you'll live on one kidney. I'm told that hurts a lot."

Hardesty's expression didn't change. "You don't leave me much. Ellsworth will have me shot anyway."

"So which is it?"

"Neither," Hardesty said. "I've lost nothing in this chickenshit outfit. Take me with you on the way out."

"We can't trust you," Sarge said.

"Why not? I'm a convict, same as this one. Pittson, aren't you? Sure you are, put two tough creeps in sick bay. I remember you. Look, I can do some farming. After you've seen Mr. Farr, you'll know why I'd just as soon go with you. He always treated me decently, and I had no hand in what they did to him."

"Did to him?" Sarge said. "Did what?"

"You'll see. You may need me to carry him. I don't think he'll be walking."

"Jesus," Sarge said. He looked at the clock over the desk. Not much past midnight. "What do you think, Garrett?"

I shrugged. "We got much choice?"

"Guess not. Okay, Hardesty, do it. If you play tricks on us, God help you."

"And you'll take me with you."

"Yes."

"If you don't know how to work the intercom, you'll have to untie me." Sarge and I exchanged looks. Then I loosened the cords. Hardesty scooted his chair over to the intercom and punched buttons. "Carruthers."

"Yes, sergeant."

"Bring Farr up to his office. He conscious?"

"Kind of. Mr. Ellsworth said to soften him up some more."

"You'll get your fun later. I need the bastard to help find things up here. Bring him."

"Okay. Your responsibility."

We waited. "How many will come?" Sarge asked.

"Two."

"Get down behind the desk, Garrett. I'll stay by the door. If Hardesty does anything funny, shoot him in the balls."

"Right." I crouched, and Hardesty rolled up to sit at the desk. "Keep your hands in sight," I told him. We waited some more.

They knocked at the door.

"Come," Hardesty said.

The door opened, and two men pushed a wheelchair through. As they got inside, Sarge kicked the door shut. I came out from behind the desk.

"What the hell?" The guard had no time to say anything else. I smashed his face with the barrel of my pistol, got my hand over his mouth, and chopped down, twice, at the base of his skull.

Then I had time to look up and see how Sarge was doing. He was wiping his knife on the other guard's coveralls. "Mine's finished," he said. "Yours?"

"Near enough."

"Finish him."

I hesitated a moment. I'd never killed anyone before. I'd been ready to, in fights, but it had never happened, and this guy was helpless. While I stood there, Sarge came over and cut his throat. "Dead he's no problem," he said. "Jesus, Skipper, what have they done to you?"

Farr mumbled something, but we couldn't understand him. Sarge turned on Hardesty. The guard was still sitting at the desk, his hands on top in plain sight.

"Skipper, did this creep do this to you?" Sarge demanded.

"Aagh. No," Farr said. He had trouble talking, because there were new gaps in his teeth, and his lips were swollen to three times their normal size. One eye was closed, and the other bled. He tried to get up, but couldn't. Then he swallowed hard. "Hardesty is okay," he mumbled.

They had taken Farr's p-suit, and of course he had no helmet. "How do we get him out of here?" I asked. If we could get one of the school's practice suits, we might get that on him."

"Yeah," Sarge said. "Hardesty, how do we do that?"

"Beats me. Nobody's going to bring one here. Won't be long before somebody wonders what happened to Carruthers. And I'm supposed to make night rounds in a half hour."

"Crap doodle," Sarge said. "We've got a skintight hid in the corridor, but he wouldn't live a minute, not bunged up the way he is. We've got to get one of those EVA jobs."

"Carry him in a pressure sack," Hardesty said.

"And where the hell do we get a pressure sack?" Sarge demanded.

"Kitchen," Commander Farr mumbled. "Plenty in there."

"It'll be locked," Hardesty said. "I've got the keys. Right here." He pointed to the table where we'd put everything we'd found in his pockets.

I thought for a moment, then began peeling off layers of clothing. "We'll go together, Hardesty. You and me."

"Fine."

"Garrett, I still don't trust him," Sarge said.

"Got a better plan?"

"No."

It turned out to be no trouble at all. The night kitchen staff were used to Hardesty's midnight raids. He'd been running a black market operation in Hellastown, selling food stolen from the school kitchens and splitting with the cooks.

When we got back we dressed Farr in all my spare clothes and put him in the sack with an oxygen bottle. Then we locked the office door and went through the passageway back to the astronomy section. When we got there, Sarge went through into the dome, and came back a minute later with two prisoners.

"What is the meaning of this?" She was a gray-haired woman. I'd seen her pictures in the papers, a Nobel Prize winner. Lady Elizabeth Murray. I couldn't remember what she got the prize for, something about the shape of the universe.

"We need some outside travel gear," Sarge said. He turned to the other astronomer, a young man in his twenties. "You like that telescope out there?" Sarge demanded.

"Why yes, of course." He didn't seem very nervous about the situation.

"What do you think a grenade would do to the mirror?"

"Good God, you can't be serious!" the man said.

"I can be. You go find us some outside gear for these two." He indicated Hardesty and me. "Garrett, you go with him. I'll keep the lady here with us. And if you're not back in five minutes, mister, that eye is going out."

"I would rather you threatened *me,*" Lady Elizabeth said.

"Yeah, I thought so," Sarge told her. "Well?"

"Do as he says, Dereck," Lady Elizabeth said. "I believe he means it."

"There's a locker room just here," Dereck told me. He led me down the corridor and through a door. "I say, what is this all about?"

"I'm not sure myself," I told him. "You're in no danger. We just want to get the hell out of here."

"You're welcome to go. You've cost us a prime night of observation, you know. We're looking for a new planet. Lady Elizabeth knows where it must be, and tonight will be perfect for finding it."

He opened the door to the locker room. There was a lot of gear hanging on the wall. I grabbed stuff I thought would fit me, then more for Hardesty. "Let's go," I said.

It took more time to get the cold-weather gear on. We were just getting dressed when we heard alarm bells.

11

"Into the lock. Quick!" Sarge barked.

"What about them?" I pointed to our scientist prisoners.

"Leave 'em. You two want your eye to keep lookin', you better pray we're out before the guards get here. Move!"

We carried Farr into the air lock. While it was cycling, Sarge reached into the sack and set the regulator to four pounds. That should be enough pure oxygen, if the bottle didn't freeze. It had no heater system like the ones in our suits. We had it inside Farr's jacket to help keep it warm. He was breathing, but we didn't think he could manage for himself.

The outer door opened and we bolted for the ladder. Technicians looked up from their consoles. We couldn't see expressions through their faceplates, but they *must* have wondered what the hell we were doing.

Sarge swarmed up the ladder, then threw down a line. I knotted a cradle around Farr and Sarge hoisted. I waved Hardesty up next. He pushed from below while Sarge pulled. Then I started up after them.

When we reached the balcony, I thought we were safe. Sarge and Hardesty carried Mr. Farr around to the big gap the telescope looked through, and went on to the outside balcony.

Then the air-lock door opened and marines swarmed through. They had p-suits and coveralls, but no cold-weather gear; they wouldn't be out here long. Without all my extra gear I was feeling the cold myself, despite the exertion of climbing.

They raised their rifles and orange flashes spurted silently. I drew my pistol and fired back, also in silence. No hits for either side. Then I was through to the outside balcony. By then Sarge had lowered Mr. Farr over the side, and he and Hardesty were busy paying out line. I stopped at the slit where I could cover the ladder.

Unlike me, the marines had very little target to shoot at. I saved my ammunition until one of them reached the ladder then took very careful aim and shot him off it. Two of his buddies ran over and picked him up. They were brave men. I held my fire; they were no threat to us, and the more tied down taking care of the wounded, the better for me.

"Okay, kid!" Sarge called. The voice was loud in my helmet radio.

"Right." I waited a little longer, on the theory that the marines might have been listening. They had been. Three of them rushed the ladder. I shot the leading one and he fell, carrying the two below back to the floor. Something tugged at my right sleeve, and I looked down. There was a big rip in the coveralls and insulation, but the slug had missed me by a good two inches; that foam was thick.

I fired once more, not caring if I hit anything, and ran around the balcony. They'd be coming up the ladder any moment. It was eighty feet to the ground below. Sarge and Hardesty were running across the badlands, carrying Farr, their helmet lights dancing across the ground.

No time to go down the rope, I told myself. Eighty feet. Mars gravity is about 40 percent Earth. But it's not the same, there's a squared factor in there. No time to work it out, and the marines couldn't be far behind me.

I swung over the edge and dropped toward the ground below.

I worked it out later: I fell for almost three seconds, which seems like forever, and I hit with the same force as if I'd jumped off an eighteen-foot ladder back on Earth.

It hurt like hell. I hit and went on down, all the way, rolling, letting the thick foam padding absorb most of the force, but I still felt as if my ankles had been rammed up to my knees.

I could get up, though. It hurt, but I could run. I ran like hell toward the tractor.

We threw Mr. Farr into the bunk and Sarge climbed in with him. I put Hardesty between Chris Martin and myself in the front seat. Chris had the tractor bouncing across the rocks before we got pressure up in the cab.

"Nearest tractor air-lock is a good five kilometers from here," Sarge said.

"The Marines didn't have cold-weather gear," I told him. "They've probably gone in by now." I could still feel the cold, despite everything I'd worn. "How is Mr. Farr?"

"He's alive," Sarge growled. "Chris, get us out into the Basin. They'll never find us out there. Then head cross country for Ice Hill."

"Right. How'd it go?"

"Piece of cake." Sarge said.

* * *

They had five prisoners and one repairable tractor at Ice Hill. The other Federation tractor had been dynamited.

"Nothing to it," Sam Hendrix told us. "Their first warning that we would resist came when the leading tractor ran over ten sticks of 60 percent nitro. We had very little trouble with the second."

We got Mr. Farr inside. Erica was waiting for me. "Are you all right?"

"Piece of cake." It felt good to be able to kiss her. "And you?"

"Johnny and Ezra stopped at Windhome on the way. We picked up the two marines they left behind. Just as well for them, there was no one to get them and they would have run out of air." She took my hand. "There's a meeting in a few minutes. We're supposed to go. But we have a little time first . . . "

Commander Farr was propped up on a portable cot. Ruth Hendrix didn't want him to talk, but he insisted on having us all meet in the main hall. His voice was weak and his words tended to come out slurred, but he was all business.

"It's started," he said. "There's no turning back for any of us. Sam, did you get the word out?"

"Yes. The Rim is boiling mad. Ellsworth sent out three tanks today, but they did not go past Iron Gap. Instead they escorted the police van back, and Ellsworth has been sending messages to Marsport demanding help."

"Will he get it?"

Sam shook his head. "I do not think so. Not immediately. Some of our people in the north have begun sabotage raids. The monorail south has been cut in four places. Katrinkadorp is in revolt. They will need their marines up there for a while, I think."

"Then there's been a general revolt?" Farr demanded.

"No. Except in Katrinkadorp there is no uprising. Just our people, and sabotage."

Farr nodded to himself. "Independence. They want a meeting of the leaders. Committees and debates. Is this the proper time?" He sighed deeply. "Well, we've got no choice. We've got to do something to stir up the others."

There was a long silence. Erica took my hand. We stood, waiting for someone to say something, but no one did.

"It's too early," Farr muttered. "Everything only half planned. So we make do with what we have. The Rim is ours?"

"Yes," Sam said. "Solidly, I think. Ellsworth has done our work for us, here. We had doubters, even after the destruction of Windhome, but Mr. Ellsworth has told the Hellas Region Council that he intends to close all the stations and eliminate this rebellion once and for all. One of our people had a bug in the Council Chamber, and we have been broadcasting his speech all day. Yes, we certainly hold the Rim."

"Then we must defend it, and that means denying Ellsworth knowledge of our movements. Sarge, did you make the observations of the weather satellite?"

"Yes, sir."

"Where are they?" Farr asked.

100

"On a tape back at Windhome, sir."

"Send for them immediately. We need the ephemeris."

"Sir." Sarge went off to talk to John Appleby.

"Who is your best man with explosives?" Farr asked.

"Campbell, I think," Sam Hendrix said.

"Put him to work. We need something to knock down the weather satellite. Something to loft rocks into its path. It needn't be fancy."

"Yes, I think Campbell will have no trouble with that."

I thought they'd lost their minds. Knock down a *satellite?* With a homemade interceptor? Michael Hendrix explained it to me later. It wasn't really very difficult at all. We knew exactly where the satellite would be at any moment, and in Mars' low gravity it didn't take a very big sounding rocket to loft a bunch of rocks up the ninety kilometers where the satellite would be. The spy-eye was moving at better than three kilometers a second, and when it ran into a cloud of rock . . .

They knocked it out the next day. It didn't fall, of course, but the electronics were knocked to smash. It wouldn't be sending down any pictures of tractors moving around the Rim. And since we held the high ground above the Basin, we could see them coming any time, while they had no idea of what we were doing.

If the Federation could have got a big force together in the first week of the Revolution, that would have been the end of it; but they couldn't. There aren't any airplanes on Mars. Everything has to move by rail or by tractors, and although we didn't have any large force around Marsport, we had enough to knock out a rail line running unprotected for two thousand kilometers. We had only to deal with the two battalions of Federation troops in Hellas Region, and we had more men than they did. For the moment they could count on company cops to control the town; but the miners were seething, waiting for a spark to set them off, and Ellsworth knew it, so he wanted to keep his troops close to home.

We intercepted plenty of his messages. He was worried: there'd been no word from Major Bielenson's expedition beyond the return of the two cops who'd had Sarge. If we could swallow a dozen men, maybe we could beat a couple of hundred, too; he wasn't going to risk it until he had reinforcements from Marsport, and Marsport wasn't sending any until they were sure the capital was secure. . .

We got through the first week because Ellsworth was no more ready for war than we had been. During the second week he sent a force out, and we had a sharp battle west of Iron Gap: dynamite bombs against tanks and guns. We didn't try to hold ground west of the Gap; instead we made them fight for every meter.

The contest wasn't as unequal as it sounds. The ground was rugged, with almost no visibility. We had a few captured rifles, and after the first week we had crossbows powered by steel tractor springs. The steel quarrels would penetrate anything except plate armor and had a range almost as good as a rifle: no air, and low gravity.

We lost four men and two women. They took Chris Martin's station, but they paid for it with eight tanks and crews; and we stopped them at the Gap.

That night we made harassing raids. It was a nightmare time, with us on foot in the Martian night; but we could live outside, day or night, if we had to. We knew how. They didn't. When they lost more men in our night raid than they had in the battle, they decided they'd had enough for a while, and withdrew back to Chris Martin's place.

We were holding the Rim, but we knew we couldn't hold it forever; we needed the spark that would set all of Mars afire. And we had to find it before they sent Ellsworth enough troops to roll over us.

12

I didn't see much of Erica after the first week of the rebellion. I was assigned to Sarge's militia company and stationed at Windhome. We were the reserve unit in case Ellsworth tried to force the Gap; the advance group was holding Zeke Terman's station.

Erica had other duties, and they kept her at Ice Hill despite her protests. She was, they said, too valuable to use as a foot soldier; she knew more about power plant operations than almost anyone else, and when she didn't have power plant duties, they could use her skills as an agronomist. Food production had to be kept up. The mine camps and refineries needed all we could grow.

Bielenson hadn't had time for systematic destruction of Windhome. He'd blown out the air locks and cracked all the domes, so that everything in the station was dead, but the electronic gear was mostly untouched. I spent my time getting the solar-cell production system back into operation. We needed all the solar cells we could get. We also built fortifications, planted mines in all the approaches, and put out patrols to watch for Feddies. It didn't leave much time for anything else.

The Skipper sent for me in the third week. He was still at Ice Hill, slowly recovering from the beating he'd got.

103

Ellsworth had supervised that himself. They gave me a few hours with Erica, and even found someone to cover for her duties during that afternoon. Then I was ushered into Sam's study. The comfortable room was now general headquarters for Free Mars—what little there was of it. There were maps on all the walls, and extra communications gear had been moved in. The Skipper was able to sit in a chair, although Ruth Hendrix wouldn't let him stay up for more than a few hours a day.

Erica insisted on coming in with me. When one of the guards objected, she pushed him aside. "This is still my home, Brent Callahan, and if you think you can keep me out of my father's study, you just try it!"

"Let her come," Farr called from inside. "Good afternoon, Erica. Garrett. Please sit down. Drink?"

Erica looked at him suspiciously. "You want something."

Farr sighed. "Yes, of course I do. Does that mean I can't be civil?"

"No. . ."

"Very well. Please sit down and have a drink with me. Garrett, how do you think the war is going?"

"Sir? You'd know better than me. We seem to be holding on.

"Precisely," Farr said. "We seem to be holding on. But only holding on, and that is fatal. Part of Mars can never be independent. We must liberate the entire planet, towns and all, or we must give up."

I didn't say anything. He was right. Station holders, Rimrats around Hellas, the Afrikaners at Katrinkadorp, and all the other Marsmen like to say we can get along without the towns, but the truth is we need the heavy industry. Mars is just too hostile a place to live without some concentration of industry and power. For that matter, we still need imports from Earth, although not very many, and we could survive without them. Barely.

"I'd think the miners would join us," I said.

"They would, if they thought they could win," Commander Farr said. "We have only to give the word and there will be widespread rioting in most of the cities. In the confusion we might seize control. There are very few Federation Marines on Mars, and the company police cannot fight a mass insurrection. Assume we have done that. Then what? What will the Federation Council on Earth do?"

I shrugged. "Send troops?"

Farr nodded. "Probably. And worse. Send ships with nuclear weapons. Bomb one of our cities and invite the others to surrender."

"So why haven't they done that already?" Erica demanded.

Farr laughed. "It would cost too much, and for what? So far, Free Mars consists of the Rim and Katrinkadorp. The governor in Marsport is hardly likely to exaggerate how serious the situation is. It would be a confession of failure. And as long as we do *not* cause widespread rebellion, he won't ask for help."

"Then it's hopeless," I said. "We can't fight what they've got here unless we take the cities, and if we take the cities they'll send something we can't fight at all—"

"Your appreciation is correct, but the situation is not hopeless. The problem is hardly new. We planned to deal with it, we *had* to, before we could even contemplate independence. Unfortunately, events caught up with us. We cannot use the original plan. But there is a way."

"I don't like this," Erica said.

"I beg your pardon?"

"You heard me, Mr. Farr. I don't like this. There's no reason why you should be discussin' high policy with Garrett."

Farr merely nodded. "As you suppose, I need him."

"For something damned dangerous," Erica said. "Why Garrett?"

"Ricky!" I said.

"Don't Ricky me! You've done enough. Mr. Farr, there must be lots of people you can send."

"Unfortunately, there are not. Garrett has special qualifications for this job—"

"Crap!" I'd never seen Erica so angry. "What's so damned special about Garrett? Me, I happen to love the guy, but how's he special to you?"

"I can't tell you. No hint of this must ever get out. Only those going on the mission will know."

"You can find somebody else! We're going to be married, and Garrett has done enough."

I had been just about to say the same thing. I really

had. Why should I volunteer? But I wasn't going to have my red-headed, blue-eyed sweetheart make a coward out of me in front of the commanding officer! Even then, I might still have told him to find another boy, but she started talking at the same time I did, and I heard myself say, "I'll do it, Commander. What do you need?"

I heard myself say it. I put it that way because it was *not* what I'd intended to say. I am not a hero.

It took another ten minutes to get Ricky out of the office.

By the time she was gone, we weren't speaking. She'd told me I was a damned fool, and I felt like one. "All right, sir, what the hell is so special about me?" I demanded.

"You're less than a Mars year from Earth," Farr said. He pointed to a big map on the wall next to him. "There is one thing we can do that will assure that Earth won't interfere, and also spark the townsmen into revolution. We must begin the Project."

I thought he'd gone off his head. I told him so.

"Not at all."

"But that takes atom bombs," I said. "Anyway that's what they tell me—"

"It does. You're going to get them for us."

"Now I know you've lost your mind. Sir."

"I assure you I haven't," Farr said. "How do you make an atomic bomb?"

"Good Lord, I don't know. That's a secret—"

"Hardly. Any high school student could find out. The basic structure of nuclear weapons has been known, and published, since 1949. An atomic weapon is nothing more than a critical mass of the proper radioactive materials. The only difficult part is obtaining the fissionables, such as refined uranium. And there is plenty of refined uranium on Mars."

"And you want me to walk in and steal some?"

Farr grinned. It wasn't a pleasant grin because of the gaps in his teeth. "How did you guess? That happens to be precisely what I want you to do. Now look here on this map.

"The Federation, not being entirely insane, keeps all refined uranium in a safe place. Specifically here, in this crater." He pointed to one of the big rimwalls in the

Deucalion region. The crater was over a hundred and fifty kilometers in diameter.

"It happens that the main industrial power pile for Novoya Sverdlovsk and Marspot is also in Deucalion Crater," Farr said. "Thus, if we take control of this installation, we have the materials for atomic weapons, and also a very big threat to use against the major companies. We give the companies a choice: help us, or lose their power supply."

"That makes sense," I said. Solar power is marvelous but on the scale the big outfits operate on it takes a lot more than they can collect with solar cells. Only the big atomic power plants can furnish the kind of power Mars General and the other big industries need.

I looked at the map. The power plant and uranium storage facility were located right in the center of the crater. A monorail line ran from there to the crater rim, then branched, one branch running north to Novoya Sverdlovsk in Edom Crater, the other directly east to Yappy Crater and Marsport. There was no other way in. "How do we get there?" I asked. "They can see us coming for—"

"For about 250 kilometers," Farr said. "Obviously we cannot take them by surprise if we use the monorails. The trains are stopped at the rim, and there is a large garrison there. Even if we could capture a train without causing an alarm, which I doubt, we wouldn't get past that garrison."

"Yeah, but if we take tractors there's no way we can get into the crater without being seen, and certainly no way to get across it. That's smooth plain, not a big boulder field like Hellas—"

"I see you appreciate the problem," Farr said. "Actually, it's worse than that. There are observation posts all around the rim. A tractor couldn't get within a hundred miles of Deucalion crater without being spotted."

He was enjoying this. "Then I don't see how we do it. Wait a minute. You said walk." I looked at the map again. "Commander, you're talking about going 150 miles *on foot?*"

"Yes."

"Can't be done. A man can't carry enough air, let

alone food and water. Be generous; figure we make forty miles a day—"

"I think you would average more like twenty."

"So do I. Call it thirty. That's five days and it's just not possible."

"I sincerely hope the Feddies think that way," Farr said. "And I rather suppose they do. Most of their officials have not been here very long. Men who live on Mars tend to become Mars sympathizers, meaning they are unreliable and thus not to be trusted around the uranium stockpile. If you, with all your Rim experience, think it can't be done, then I'm sure they think that."

I looked at the map again, then shook my head. "I don't see it. Sure, if you can guarantee us permafrost near the surface, maybe, just maybe, we could carry enough solar cells to set up airmakers and hydrolize water to get oxygen. But we'd spend one day out of two just sitting there collecting power, and it'd take damn near an acre of solar cells. It'd be easier to hide tractors!"

"Right again. Nevertheless, there is a way. Give up?"

"Yeah," I said. "I give up. How?"

He told me. I leaned back in my chair and laughed like hell. Then I stopped laughing. I was going to have to do it.

* * *

Five hundred men and seventy tractors: not a very large military force on which to pin the hopes of a world. At that it was 20 percent of the Rim's fighting strength. We had to be very careful not to be seen, because if Ellsworth knew the Rim had sent that much force to the north, he could attack without much fear.

Our agents in Hellastown were instructed to foment sabotage and rebellion among the miners; incidents, work slowdowns, riots, anything to keep Ellsworth on edge and his troops in town. Meanwhile our group started northwest.

We crossed the Rim Range by a track that led past my valley. I had never seen it except on maps, but I recognized it, a big ringwall and two small flat-top mesas, with a canyon below them. I stared at it, wondering if I would ever live there with Erica. It seemed such a short time ago that we were planning where to put our agro-domes, and where our first tunnel would be.

It *was* a short time, I told myself. Less than a month. Yet, although it seemed that we'd been engaged only a few days, the month of war seemed like a year. Time is a strange thing, and I'm not at all sure we understand it as well as we think we do.

We went under the monorail from Hellastown to Marsport by passing through a deep canyon at night. When that was behind us we all breathed a sigh of relief. Then we plunged on across the plains, across canyon ends, over craters or around them, striving for a straight-line distance of a hundred miles a day. The way was tortuous; we often had to drive twice a hundred miles and more to do it. We had no real maps, only satellite photographs; no one had ever been here before us.

Since we couldn't possibly carry enough air and water with us, scout groups went ahead to find ice caves and permafrost. The scouts were old Rimrat prospectors who knew what to look for, men with years of experience at interpreting tiny shadows and vague marks on photographs. Without their abilities we could never have crossed thirteen hundred miles at all, much less in fifteen days.

When they found water the scouts set up solar-cell arrays to power airmakers—out here we didn't worry about being seen. Although the Federation had a manned ship in orbit, after the weather satellite was knocked out they moved it up to almost two thousand miles above the surface. Even with a good telescope aimed precisely where we were they'd have been lucky to find us, and Farr gave them something else to look at by sending meaningless expeditions out into Hellas Basin.

The landscape was bleak and empty except for the blowing red dust that's everywhere on Mars when there's wind. We crossed vast boulder-strewn plains, saw flat-topped mesas in the distance, and always there was that dark sky with wispy clouds and dust plumes rising into it, and the pink sky at the horizon. We went around craters and mountains, over rimwalls, and still we moved on.

There was one large canyon, over a kilometer wide and two hundred meters deep. We couldn't go around it, and there was no way for a tractor to crawl down inside it. Instead, we anchored a crane at the top and lowered our tractors and all but five of the men. The five took the crane apart, lowered the pieces, and climbed down. Then we crossed the canyon, and five of us climbed the opposite wall. We dropped a light line and used that to pull up a heavy cable. Then for two days we pulled up, by hand, our disassembled crane.

When it was assembled on the canyon lip, one tractor on the canyon floor was used to haul the others, one by one, straight up the side of that sheer cliff. Once the cable failed, and a tractor tumbled out of the sling to smash itself to bits on the rocks below. The next tractor went up full of men.

We went on, through sandstorms and hurricanes. Fifteen days after we left the Rim we were just under a hundred miles south of Deucalion Crater. We set up our base camp there.

The main force was commanded by an old Rimrat named Hiram Zemansky who had been an engineer on Earth; there seemed to be nothing he couldn't do. I had my final conference with him at dawn in the big pressure tent with an air lock we had set up as a command post. His group would keep the tractors, and they were in no hurry.

My own command waited outside. There were forty of us, all young men, and all, like me, less than a Mars year from Earth. Some had been apprentice Marsmen in other stations. The rest were escapees fleeing labor contracts. They weren't devoted to the cause of independence—they weren't devoted to anything. But they said they wanted to fight, and they were young and tough. We needed them.

The plan was to walk in—if we could. Being accustomed to Earth gravity, we could carry nearly twice as much as the old-timers and those born on Mars, but that wouldn't be enough; we could carry only three days' supplies, and we had a hundred and fifty miles to go, with a battle at the end of the trek.

"Call it nine days," I told Hiram. "That leaves us a little time to get into position. If all goes well, we'll hit them at dawn on the ninth day from now."

"Right." He grinned at me, but there wasn't much humor in it. "Think you can handle that bunch?" he asked.

I shrugged. "They're not much different from Dog Soldiers. We'll get by." There was nothing more to say. I took a letter from my pouch and handed it to Zemansky. "See that Erica Hendrix gets this if I don't get back."

"Sure. You'll be back."

"Yeah. Piece of cake."

"You give the signal and we'll come a-runnin'," Hiram said. "You'll be back home in a month."

"Sure. Okay, here we go." I went out to where my command was waiting for me.

Our packs lay on the ground. They were enormous. When we'd practiced this back at Ice Hill and I'd first seen what we were supposed to carry, I thought the Skipper had gone crazy. When I got that thing hoisted onto my shoulders, I was sure of it.

"Load up," I said. We sat on the ground and struggled into the straps, then gingerly got to our feet. The camp looked very comfortable. The journey by tractor had been miserable, but now, under that load, I was already beginning to miss it.

"Move out." I waved forward, toward the north. We began the long march.

We walked in silence. I could hear grunts from the men, but even at the start we didn't have much breath to waste on conversation. Our radios were set to the lowest power, only a couple of hundred meters range, and as the column strung out many of the troops were isolated from everyone except their partners; we marched in a three-man buddy system. "One to break his leg, one to stay with him, and one to go for help."

We picked our way in single file, our three-man groups strung out over a kilometer of flat terrain broken by boulders and small craters. From the top of an occasional gentle rise we could see the rim of Deucalion ahead of us, but most of the time there was nothing but the next rock, or the helmet of the man in front of you.

Within minutes my legs felt ready to give out. Those packs were *heavy!* It takes a hundred pounds of equipment just to keep a man alive on Mars: air pressure regulator and recycler; pressure suit and helmet; insulated clothing; your share of a five-man pressure tent for shelter at night and at meal times; sleeping bag; batteries. Another 36 pounds a day per man of expendables: food, water, air, and air tankage. Three days worth is 108 pounds—208 pounds per backpack.

In Mars gravity that's only 80 pounds. I kept telling myself that. Soldiers on Earth used to carry that much. The Foreign Legionnaires marched into battle with 90 pounds. But ours had the *mass* of 208 pounds. When you get that moving, it *keeps* moving. It's as if you had to push a washing machine across an ice pond.

We carried few weapons. We'd get those the same way we'd get our supplies. If the air and water didn't come through, we wouldn't need weapons.

I sang to myself. After a while some of the others joined in. "It s eighty-six miles to water, my lads, it's ninety-nine more to beer, if I hadn't been born a damn bloody fool, I'd not be a volunteer." Left. Right.

Break for ten minutes every hour. Across the level stretches we can make five kilometers in fifty minutes. Lie down on the breaks, you need the rest. Wait for stragglers to catch up. If you don't keep up, your break is shorter. Keep an eye on your watch; it's easy to stay down too long, and you'll stiffen up. That's it. Up again, and move on.

We were faceless men under our helmets. When we moved out we looked like huge packs with legs. I knew them all by name, but little else. Don Plemmons, my second in command. Lonny Wilson, a kid from Washington, D.C.—almost a neighbor, he'd heard of the Dog Soldiers! —who'd been one of Commander Farr's last recruits and was scheduled to move in with me when I set up station in the valley I still thought of as my own.

Left. Right. Sing again. "When John Henry was a little baby, sittin' on his mammy's knee, he said that Big Bend tunnel on the C&O road is gonna cause the death of me, Lord God! gonna cause the death of me . . ." Left. Right.

The day ended, somehow. Eight hours of marching. A little over twenty-three miles. We set up camp in a hollow out of the wind and collapsed, too tired even to eat.

If they had a chance they'd go back. I knew that. If they got together and talked it over they'd turn back. But one can't go back alone. Two can't. If any go on, all go on, because they were men and men have pride.

Wilson told me the four others in his tent were ready to quit. He didn't say more.

"And you?" I asked.

He just looked at me. I recognized the expression. It was just the way I used to look at the older members, back when I first joined the Dog Soldiers and had pride in my gang. *I am as tough as you,* the look said. He cleared his throat. "I'm game."

I wasn't. But how could I go back? I'd said I'd lead this damned-fool expedition. Erica would be glad to see me—but how could I face Sarge? How could I face me? I couldn't crawl home and admit defeat now. Not after I said I could do it. "Break camp and load up."

Wilson went out to hustle the others. The sun was an hour high when we started. We looked back longingly toward the horizon to the south, but when I turned north they followed. First Wilson, then the others, three by three.

At noon we reached the point of no return. We were a day and a half from the base camp, half our air gone. If we went on from here we were committed. An irrevocable decision. A nice word, that: irrevocable. No outs. No turning back, unless you turn back now, this minute, this second—

I didn't halt. This was not even time for a break. By the time I let them stop to rest—let us, let *myself* stop to rest —there was nothing for it but to go on. Committed. Irrevocable.

Shortly after we got moving again we came to a deep chasm, thirty meters wide, a hundred deep, stretching as far as we could see to either side. A grapnel flung across it caught on the third try. Wilson shed his pack and swarmed across hand-over-hand, dangling above the canyon floor, swaying in the wind—

He made it. God knows how. More lines were thrown, and soon we had a rope bridge. Wilson had to come back for his pack. No one could possibly have carried it for him. The wind swayed the bridge, and my pack was enormously heavy as I shuffled, one foot at a time, over the narrow gorge.

It was still relatively level terrain. Tomorrow will be the worst, I told myself. How can it get any worse than this?

113

Left. Right. Sing, damn you! "Now the Cap'n said to Johnny Henry, gonna bring me a steam drill 'round, gonna take that steam drill out on the job, gonna hammer the mountains right down, Lord God, gonna hammer the mountains right down. And John Henry said ·to that Cap'n, and there was fire a-flashin' in his eye, with a twelve-pound hammer and a four-foot handle, gonna beat your steam drill or I'll die, Lord God. . . ." Left. Right.

Camp at dusk. Inflate the tents. Put the dehydrated food to soaking. You'll eat it cold, there's no heat. Everyone inside, into sleeping bags, before the chill sets in. Eat, and lie back on the rocky ground.

The packs were lighter the next day. We had used two days' supplies, seventy Earth pounds, almost half the weight we carried. There was another gorge ahead of us, but we crossed it easily. Sing happier songs. The rhythm of the trail, get into it, you've got a fifty-pound pack and no worries, so it's uphill now, so what? When we crossed the gorge, we were at the edge of Deucalion crater.

Like most craters, Deucalion slopes gently outward. The inner face is sheer cliff. That would be a problem when we came to it. For now, onward and upward. "And the white man said to John Henry, black man damn your soul, you're going to beat that drill of mine when the rocks in the mountains turn to gold, Lord God, when the rocks in the mountains turn to gold. And John Henry say to that white man, Lord a man ain't nothin' but a man, but before I let your steam drill beat me down, gonna die with my hammer in my hand, Lord God. . . "

Pick up the pace. This is the critical day. Today we have to climb high enough to be in line-of-sight back to Zemansky's group, or we have had it.

Damn fool stunt, Garrett. Damn fool. Left. Right. "And John Henry said to his shaker, black man why don't you sing, I'm a-slingin' twelve pounds from my hips on down, just you listen to that cold steel ring, Lord God, just you listen to that cold steel ring. . . "

We made camp at dusk. Just before dark I set up the signal laser on its tripod and aimed it precisely at the top of a flat mesa three days march behind us. I opened the focus out as far as it would go, and played it across the eastern edge of the tabletop forty miles away.

Wilson crouched beside me, his helmet touching mine. "Be like the bastards to be off playing cards."

"That'd fix us," I said. I tongued the mike button. "Big Momma, this is John Henry. Over."

Nothing. I tried again. And again.

"There." Wilson was shouting. "There, I saw it! Flash of light!"

"Maybe." Our photophone target was only a meter in diameter. I slaved our transmitter to our target and waited. Forty miles away Zemansky's troops played their transmitter across our area. When their beam hit our target, our unit sent back a response; with time they would be able to focus in, setting their transmission unit in micrometer steps until it was precisely aimed at our reflector, then narrow the focus. "Maybe."

"Cheep." It was one of the loveliest sounds I had ever heard, the tone that indicated they'd touched our target with their beam. "Cheep . . . cheep . . . cheep, cheep, cheep cheep cheepcheepcheep—Hello John Henry, this is Big Mama. Do you read us? Over."

I stood and gave the victory signal, hands together over my head. The men around me were cheering, I knew, but I couldn't hear them. We were in radio silence.

"Big Mama I hear you. I read you three by four, over."

"Stand by John Henry, incoming mail at twenty-three hundred hours, I say again, twenty-three hundred hours. Godspeed. Big Mama out."

"So we wait some more," I told Wilson.

He nodded, but there was a grin a mile wide on his face. I only then realized that he hadn't believed this would work.

I still wasn't so sure it would.

13

I was exhausted, but I couldn't sleep. Neither could the others. We had air to last until morning. The two hours until twenty-three hundred dragged on, and on.

Back at base camp they would have us located exactly. The survey laser was slaved to their communication unit; once they had it aimed at us, they had direction and range within centimeters. I lay back in my sleeping bag imagining what was happening on the mesa forty miles to the south.

Eighteen hundred pounds of supplies loaded into the rocket. Ceramic tanks of alcohol and oxygen for propellant. Everything was made of ceramic and fiberglass, everything that could be, so that when the rocket tripped the radar scanners on Deucalion rim above us, it would look to the Feddie observers like nothing more than a meteroid coming in at a shallow angle.

It would never have worked on Earth.

I wondered if it would work here. It was a bit late for that question. Twenty-three hundred hours. We watched, and I listened.

"John Henry, this is Big Mama."

"Big Mama, go."

"On the way."

We saw nothing, of course; the bird didn't need a lot of power to fling it forty miles. It burned out a few seconds after it was launched.

We waited another minute. "It's there," Big Mama said.

We were ready. A dozen men were suited up and went out searching with radio receivers. The homing signal the supply rocket sent was deliberately weak, carrying no more than a few hundred meters at most.

Wait some more. Then one of the troops was running toward me. He came up and gestured. The victory signal.

We had supplies for three more days.

The next day was the worst of all. Our packs were full again, and we were climbing uphill. Each step was agony. Onward and upward. Left. Right. But by God we were going to make it! "John Henry say to that Cap'n, looky yonder what I do see, well your hole done choke and your drill done broke, and you can't drive steel like me! Lord God, you can't drive steel like me!"

In late afternoon we made camp below the rim. There was a Feddie observation post no more than two kilometers away. We knew that from the map, but we never saw it. We crossed the rim at night, when Phobos was up high enough to give light to the weird landscape around us. I left four men and supplies at the lip; they were our signal relay station. Then we strung lines and lowered ourselves into Deucalion crater.

We made camp after midnight, and we were up at dawn, but now we were confident. At the bottom of the cliffs we divided our already tiny force. Plemmons and nine men angled off to the right, headed for the monorail that ran from the rim to the storage area. My group kept on straight ahead.

It wasn't a smooth plain. There were rocks and boulders, and the crater floor was cracked and broken. We picked our way across, glad of the wind and dust that made us invisible to anyone above who might be looking down into the crater.

The next supply rocket was tricky: we had no direct line of sight to Zemansky. Instead we relayed through the detachment on the rim. They had survey equipment and could locate us relative to them; and they were in line of sight to the main camp. It was a simple double-offset problem, and I shouldn't have worried, but I did. I worried about everything.

The rocket almost hit us. We actually saw it fall, no more than a hundred meters away.

And on the night of the eighth day, two more: supplies and weapons. Deucalion power station was less than five kilometers ahead. We'd made it.

"Now the white man that invented that steam drill, well he thought that it was so fine, and John Henry drove in fourteen feet, and the steam drill only made nine, Lord God! and the steam drill only made nine."

* * *

It was an hour before dawn. The men were in position, and there was nothing to do but watch the second hand of my watch as it ticked toward H-hour. I watched it and recalled the last conference with Sarge and Commander Farr.

"The main garrison is at the rim," Farr had said. "The guards at the storage center itself are mostly officers, and not many of those. It has to be that way. The Feddies don't trust anyone with that kind of power. They don't think they have to, anyway. No one can get close to the depository without alerting the rim garrison. Or so they think."

"You surprise 'em, you got 'em," Sarge had added. "Just blast your way in. You won't be fightin' more than fifty people. Don't give 'em time to organize. They'll never know what hit them."

The second hand ticked over. I turned my radio to full power. "Now!"

Two dozen rocket launchers fired shaped charges at the station in front of us: air locks, tunnel walls, any exposed place. We reloaded and fired another volley. Then we rushed forward.

Wilson's group had stripped to the minimum, discarding every metal object not needed for survival, then crawled right up to the main entrance. They rushed forward with satchel charges, and dashed away again. The air-lock doors blew off. More rockets were fired into the tunnel to blow holes in the inner doors. Again Wilson's people dashed forward, and the entrance was blown open.

We poured into the tunnels. We threw grenades into every passageway, never turning a corner without throwing a grenade around it first. There was a guard room just inside the main entrance; they were still struggling into their helmets when we got inside and shot them down.

They weren't Marsmen. Half the station personnel died because they couldn't find their helmets in time. Many of them had taken off their skintights when they went to bed; these had no chance at all. We grenaded their rooms anyway.

It became a nightmare. Bloody corpses lay in the corridors, in the barracks, everywhere. We blasted open more airtight doors and threw explosives through them, then dashed down another corridor, firing as we went, yelling and screaming like madmen.

The only sound was our own screaming. Grenades exploded silently. Rifles grew momentary orange flowers, but soundlessly, soundlessly; through it all we yelled into our radios.

There is a madness that takes control of men in combat, it is an ugly madness that lets you do things that later you cannot even comprehend. I remember very little of that fight.

"Wilson. No!" I shouted. We had reached the reactor control room. The door was airtight, and Wilson was placing a plastique charge against it. I had to struggle with him. If his hands had not been occupied with the explosive, if he had held a pistol in one of them, he would have killed me.

"No," I told him. "We can give them a chance to surrender. They're the last." There was a phone jack on the bulkhead, and I plugged my helmet set into it. "Hello in there."

After a moment there was an answer. "Who the—who are you?"

"Acting Lieutenant Pittson, Free Mars Army. Will you surrender?"

"What will you do with us?" the man demanded.

"Power station technicians will operate the reactor. Everybody else will be treated as a prisoner of war. We'll be glad to send you back to Marsport as soon as exchanges can be arranged. How many of you are there?"

There was no answer.

"I'm sure you can figure out a way to kill me while I stand here talking to you," I said. "And then what? My troops will blast you out of there. If you're waiting for the rim garrison to come rescue you, forget it." I sounded a lot more confident than I was. If everything had gone well, Plemmons had cut the monorail line from the rim, and Zemansky's force was racing across the plains to reinforce us. If.

"I give you one minute," I said.

"Can we trust you?"

"That's a dumb question," I said. "You've got no choice. You have my word as a Free Mars officer that you won't be harmed if you surrender—and my word again that we can and will dig you out if we have to."

Half the minute went by. Then: "Some of us don't have suits in here. We surrender. But how can we open the door?"

"We'll manage." After the last few days, a technical problem was a relief. "We'll rig a temporary pressure wall," I said. "Wilson, get on it."

Deucalion power station was ours.

* * *

"Garrett! I've got a relay to Plemmons!" The signalman was urgently pulling me toward his radio.

"Okay. A second." I turned to the chief of the power station technicians. "All right. None of our people understands this place." I waved, indicating the control room, with its walls covered with meters and oscilloscopes, and the three big consoles that controlled the system. "But we'll know if power is not getting through to Marsport and Edom. If that power cuts out, we have no reason to hold this place. We'll blow it to hell and gone."

I turned to one of my own troopers, a nineteen-year-old from California. I spoke loud enough so the dozen prisoners could hear me. "Kehiayan, you're in charge. If they do anything funny, put 'em outside. You needn't bother with giving them air tanks."

"Rog."

"Okay, Doug, let's go."

Communications were a problem. Plemmons was out on the crater floor somewhere, a long way out of line of sight. The only way we could talk was through our relay station up on the rim.

"Barnstorm, this is John Henry, go ahead," I said.

"John Henry this is Barnstorm. We cut the monorail. A trainload of Feddies came out of the garrison when you attacked. We stopped the train, but there's two hundred of them headed your way. We can't hold 'em. We'll keep sniping the repair crews to halt the train."

"How far away?"

"We're about fifty kilometers from you. They offloaded some tractors."

"Tractors or tanks?" I asked.

"Both. I have to go, we're down to four men."

"God bless you—"

"Yeah, there's none like us. Barnstorm out."

"Get me the relay station," I told the communications man.

"John Henry, this is Relay One. Over."

"You monitor that call from Plemmons?"

"Right."

"Where's the main force?"

"Headed in at flank speed."

"Get a message to Zemansky. Have him broadcast to Marsport. We've got the power station. If they shell this place, or take it away from us, we'll blow hell out of it. If they leave us alone, we'll keep the power coming. Make sure everybody knows that. Get Mars Industries Association to understand it, too."

"Roger, John Henry."

Wilson had come up while I was talking. "Think they'll hold off?" he asked.

"Doubt it. Not now, not until they're sure they can't recover the bomb makings. How're you doing on the vault?"

"Blew open clean. What do we do with that stuff?"

"Get some of those transport containers out into the flatland, and bury 'em. Report where you've hidden them to Relay One, but don't make any maps."

Wilson eyed me narrowly. "It's that way, huh? Okay."

I took a dozen troops and went forward toward the

approaching Feddies. We had to hold them until Zemansky's group could get to us. We deployed in broken ground a kilometer from the big dome-shape of the station.

"Try to keep between them and the reactor containment," I told them. "They won't shoot heavy stuff if they think it'll wreck the power plant. They don't know how many of us there are. Keep moving, and make 'em think there's a lot."

Then we lay down and waited.

Do men love war? Certainly it is easier to fight than to think about it. What had those Feddies done to me? They were young men, like us, some with families. They'd joined up to see the world, or for the pay, or even, I suppose, because they believed in the Federation and world peace. Now they were coming to kill us, and we were waiting to kill them.

You think like that when you're waiting. You imagine a bullet tearing through your p-suit, and the blood spurting out, blood pushed by five pounds of pressure so that even veinous blood streams like a fountain. You think of what that bullet can do to you, and what the bullets in your own rifle can do to them. You wonder what the hell you're doing out here, and why you don't run like hell and let the others fight.

Such thoughts can finish you. If I had them, the others did too. "Sing, damn you," I said.

"Sing what?" someone asked.

"Anything."

Have you ever heard "The Two Grenadiers?" Why in God's name one of the troops had ever learned that, or why any of us should care about an emperor over two hundred years in his grave, I don't know; what was France to us? But it reminded us of brave men and brave deeds. We lay under the black sky of Mars, dust blowing over us, and listened.

> ". . .and under her soil to lay me,
> and when my cross on its scarlet band,
> over my heart you've bound me,
> then put my musket in my hand,
> and belt my sword around me.

So shall I lie and listen,
Aye!, keeping shield watch in my grave. . ."

Wilson came up behind me. He motioned out toward
the horizon. Was the dust thicker out there?

". . .then armed will I rise from out of my grave,
and stand as my Emperor's defender!"

"Bloody hell, what kind of song is that?" someone
shouted. "I'll give you a song!

When a man grows old,
and his balls grow cold. . ."

I recognized the voice. Hartig, who boasted that he was
the only man on Mars who knew the entire and uncut
version of "Eskimo Nell." There was no tune, but it kept
us from thinking about what was coming. It went on in-
terminably.

Wilson nudged me and pointed. The dust was defi-
nitely thicker out there. We had another twenty minutes,
no more. I thought about where I'd put the men. No
point in moving them.

". . .Oh, a moose or two,
and a caribou,
and a couple of buffalo. . ."

I'm no expert on battles and war. After that day I
never want to be. But I won't forget lying in the dust,
watching the enemy column grow larger while my ears
rang with the improbable exploits of Deadeye Dick and
Mexico Pete.

As they started to fan out, we hit the lead tank with
three rockets. It stopped, and one crewman leaped out.
He ran for shelter, and for a moment it looked as if he'd
make it, but then he fell. Deadeye Dick was at Number
Eighteen, with Eskimo Nell looking coldly on. The song
stopped. There wasn't any need for it; once the fight
starts you don't think. You just do what you have to.

The dust helped; they couldn't know how many they
were fighting. They tried to circle around us, but on that

broken ground men afoot were as fast as any tractor. And they were not Marsmen. They had been trained to fight on Earth, where they had helicopters, where a man couldn't vanish in deep shadow and be hidden five feet from you and you never know it. We crept among them, using knives in the dark shadow, leaving them to find their comrades with their hoses cut, blood spurting from their ruined lungs.

Before long they were as afraid as we were. And we couldn't run: without the power station, we'd be out of air inside a few hours. We couldn't run, but they could— as long as they had their tractors.

I realized that and we concentrated on the vehicles. Crawl through the rocks until you can get a shot at a tractor. Fire the rocket launcher and retreat, leaving the tractor disabled; and let the Feddies wonder how they'll get out when the last tractors are gone.

They moved their vehicles out of range. Now it was hand-to-hand among the broken rocks. A concentrated charge would have broken through, but they never did that. They came in little groups, trying to infiltrate.

But they could lose ten to our one, and they'd still win. We were forced back into a tighter and tighter perimeter. I had no count on how many I had left. Twenty? A dozen? I looked at my watch. Incredibly, two hours had passed since the fight had begun.

They broke past us at two places. I had no choice now. "Into the station," I ordered. We crept in, through the holes we'd blown in the tunnels earlier in the morning, and waited. It was quiet out there.

Wilson was gone. I called my communications man. "Get into the control room and tell Kehiayan to stand by. We'll have to blow this place."

"They haven't come in," Doug said. "What are they waiting for?"

"Don't know. What are *you* waiting for? Move—"

"Kind of hate to give up just now."

They still weren't coming. We were crouched in the tunnel, weapons facing the entrance. Then there was a bright flash of light out there. I could only see the light, not what caused it. There was another. Something had exploded just at the entrance. I felt the ground shake.

There was a man at the entrance. Six rifles aimed at him, but he came in with his hands high, waving the red flag of Free Mars.

The relief force had come.

14

We brought the uranium back to Ice Hill. We were
greeted as heroes. Saviors of Free Mars. So naturally
when I put in for a transfer to a nice, safe, rear-area solar
cell production facility, it was granted.

Like hell. The trouble with armies is the screwups get
the soft jobs; do something right and they tag you for
another hairy mission. To make it worse, although they
did give me a couple of weeks soft duty around Ice Hill,
it didn't do much good, because they put Erica on the
goddamn atom bomb design project. Here I went and got
their uranium and they used it as an excuse to put my
girl to work twenty-three hours a day.

We got another benefit out of Deucalion: Marsport had
to talk to us. They didn't quite recognize us as a legal
government, but what could they do? They had to have
the power from Deucalion. The Feddie government might
have thought different, but the big companies had no
doubts. They needed that power. If it took negotiating
with a bunch of criminals, then that's what it took.

We didn't need a big garrison to hold the power station. Sentries could see any attack as soon as it crossed
the crater rim—and we made sure Mars Industries As-

sociation knew what our commander's instructions were: don't fight for the station, blow it up and run like hell. Blackmail on the grand scale, but it worked.

Our raid had been successful, and something to be proud of, but it wasn't the key event of the war. While we were taking the station, another crew had captured the Federation's orbiting spaceship. Free Mars had a navy.

That was a complicated operation, carried out by Marsmen who'd had experience in space. Commander Farr had planned to lead it himself and would have if his physician had let him go; but Ruth Hendrix wasn't about to let him expose himself to six gravities.

You must start with five pounds of fuel to send one pound from Earth orbit to Mars, or vice versa. The same five pounds of fuel is needed regardless of whether the pound sent between planets is payload or ship structure, so ship designers work like mad to keep the ships light and build in no more structural strength than they need. The ships never accelerate at more than a tenth of a gravity—so why build them to stand up to more than that? That means the ships can never land. They go from orbit to orbit, but they never touch down on either Earth or Mars.

People go up to and come down from the ships by landing boat, but fuel and cargo are sent up with laser launchers. At Marsport there's a big field of lasers, all aiming into mirrors. Those mirrors are focused onto one big mirror at the end of the field. Cargo capsules ride a track onto a platform over that mirror, the lasers are turned on, and the cargo pods are shoved upward at six gravities. The space expeditionary force rode up in cargo capsules.

It was an inside job, of course. Farr and the Marsport members of the revolutionary committee had been planning it for years, placing agents in the right jobs in the spaceport, finding out which officials could be bribed, and all the rest of it. When the time came the patriots with space experience got into the capsules, rode up as cargo, and took over the ship.

It sounds simple. I'm sure it wasn't. I've heard a dozen versions of the battle for the Feddie ship, and the tamest one is enough to curl my hair. But they took her, and we now had an operational spaceship—fueled for the trip to Earth.

"That's why we've got to get working bombs," Erica said. I'd been pestering her to take some time off from work while I still had leave.

"You're going to drop atomic bombs on Earth?" I was horrified. "It's the stupidest thing I ever heard of! They'll sterilize Mars."

"We're not going to drop the bombs," Erica said. "We're going to threaten to drop the bombs. But only if they bomb us. We know we can't do any real damage to Earth—but we can knock out a big city. And we don't have to tell them which city it will be."

"Aha." I thought about that. "So every city's got a reason to argue against Feddie interference with us. Devilish. Only how do you know all this? You're not on the Committee."

"No, but I wouldn't work on the damned bombs until they told me what they were going to do with them. Would you?"

"I wouldn't work on the damn things at all. The whole idea gives me the willies. I want no part of atom bombs."

So, of course, I got sent out to explode one.

There are no airplanes on Mars. Can't be: not enough air. The usual means of transportation is by tractor or monorail. But Mars is big: half the diameter of Earth, meaning a quarter of Earth's surface area; since Earth is three-quarters covered with water, there's as much land on Mars as there is on Earth.

Most settled areas on Mars are in the southern hemisphere because southern hemisphere summers are a whack of a lot longer than northern hemisphere summers. It's not that way on Earth, but Earth has a circular orbit. Mars is closer to the sun during summer in the south. The growing season is longer, and the mine strikes were made here.

Most settlements are in the south, but not all. The most interesting scientific features are in the north: Nix Olympica, the big canyons, most active volcanoes. The first settlements in the north were scientific laboratories in the Tharsis Region, where the volcanoes are. Even in the north it's easier to live on Mars than to get here; certainly it was in the early days, so the scientists came to stay. They brought their wives and their students; after a while technicians and farmers and support people came out and stayed as well.

This was before the Federation. The first Mars settlements were founded by the United States in a cooperative effort among NASA and a lot of private foundations and universities. They didn't exactly thrive, but they were more or less self-supporting. Then the first wave of true colonists came, and the big mineral strikes were made halfway around Mars, near Hellas Rim and Edom and Iapygia where Marsport is located. The new colonies were linked together with monorails, but it was too far around to the earlier places, Livermore and New Chicago and Cal Tech's Pasadena East. Still, there had to be some means of getting from the old scientific colonies to the new commercial ones five thousand miles away. There wasn't a lot of traffic back and forth, but there was some.

If you don't have airplanes and there's no monorail, there is only one way to get across that much distance on Mars: a ballistic rocket. This isn't an airplane, although it looks a little like one. It is a reusable rocket ship with wings. It takes off on rocket power and is hurled like a bullet or a shell, traveling in free fall until it comes back into the thin Martian atmosphere and the wings can bite.

It still doesn't fly. It glides at hypersonic speed, until it has slowed down to where the pilot can turn it on its tail and let it fall toward the surface. Then he lights the rocket again and settles down gently—if everything is working. The first probes from Earth to Mars landed almost that way; the technique is hardly new.

It's a lousy system for short-range travel, but the only way to go long distances.

When Katrinkadorp rose and threw out the Feddies, there was a passenger rocket at Botha Field. After a complex series of negotiations, Commander Farr persuaded them to fly the ship down to the Rim. The reason was simple enough: Farr and the Free Mars Committee thought it wouldn't take much to bring the old university colonies into the independence movement. They wanted to send political agents to New Chicago to negotiate with the Regents who governed the scientific colonies. We had many allies, both student and faculty, and the Feddie garrison

was small. It shouldn't take much to throw out the Feddies
—but first the Regents had to be convinced that independence was possible and that the new government
wouldn't cut off their connections with their colleagues
back on Earth.

None of this concerned me. I'd heard that we had a ship
and that some of the Rim stations were working to manufacture fuel for it—liquid oxygen was no problem, we
made that every day, but rocket fuel is something else
again—but I wasn't involved.

The hell I wasn't.

I'd been hanging around Erica's workshop. I was irri-
tated because they wouldn't let me in there. Nobody but
project personnel allowed. I'd got the goddamn uranium
for them. They wouldn't *have* any project to work on if
my troops and I hadn't given ourselves a permanent case
of flat feet marching across the goddamn planet.

To top it off, Erica had been working when she wasn't
asleep, and in the little time we did have together she
acted mysterious, hinting that something big was coming
but she wouldn't tell me what. She was worried and
moody. Not much fun to be around. So we fought like
cats and dogs in the little time we had together.

If I sound a little bitter, like a neglected hero, you've
got it. If that sounds a little childish, you're right again.
So what? It was the way I felt.

So there I stood, looking for an excuse to be near the
lab in case she came out, when Perry found me. "Hey,
Garrett, the Old Man wants to see you." Then he went into the lab. *He* got to go in. He was messenger and aide to
Commander Farr. Ten-year-old kid brother gets in, but
not old Garrett.

I wandered up to the study, wondering what Farr
wanted this time, and knowing it meant a new assignment.
I'd had three weeks since I got back with the uranium. To
hell with the war, and independence, and—

Oh, I didn't mean it, of course. In the first place, if we
didn't win, my future on Mars was a little less appetizing
than the future I'd had on Earth. And I could hardly
complain about Army Mickey Mouse, because we didn't
have any. In theory I was an officer—full lieutenant, instead of just acting—and exempt from what little bullshit

there was. Not that the rank meant much. I was Lieutenant Pittson, and Sarge was just "Sarge," whatever that meant, but he sure as hell outranked me, which was as it should have been. And if anybody had tried to get some old Rimrat like Zeke Terman to salute me, it might have been interesting for a couple of minutes . . .

No, I was just unhappy because nobody paid much attention to me. I didn't have anything to do. I suspected he was about to fix that.

"Come in, Garrett," Farr said. He looked much better: the swelling was gone from around his face, and he could use his left hand a little, enough to hold a coffee cup anyway. You wouldn't have known what they'd done to him unless you saw him walking. "Have a seat."

"Yes, sir." Farr was the only one of us who rated a 'sir', and he didn't insist on it.

"We seem to be winning this war," Farr said.

"Yes, sir." That was the word we had, anyway. The Federation held the cities, but now that we had Deucalion and the orbital ship and a couple of dozen other important centers, nearly every independent station owner had come out for Free Mars. The Feddies had stopped trying to take over our territory; now they were defending what they had, and getting nervous about it at that.

"Unfortunately, there are Federation Councilors on Earth who don't believe it," Farr said. "They don't believe that we have the power to destroy an Earth city. Or they pretend they don't believe it. And they have not informed the people of Earth that we have the capability to make atomic weapons."

"But they must know we can—"

Farr shrugged. "Perhaps. Perhaps not. *You* believed it impossible. And most of the people of Earth do not know what was kept at Deucalion." He shrugged again. "There are also divisions among the miners' representatives here. Some of them are asking what is in independence for their people. Ah. Come in, Erica."

I looked around. She was a mess. She hadn't been getting enough sleep, and her eyes were red with dark bags under them. She hadn't been out of her p-suit in days, and I doubt she'd changed coveralls very recently either. Her hair was up in braids, not very flattering.

She nodded to me; we'd been fighting again.

"Well?" Farr asked.

She sank into a chair. I'd never seen her so worn out. "If the theory's right, it will work. Dr. Weinbaum says it will, anyway."

"And you think so?"

"Yes."

"Then we're ready. Do you still want to do this?"

She leaned forward, and some color came back into her face. Her eyes shone, the way they did the first night I met her. "Try and stop me!"

"I don't want to stop you. You can leave in the morning. The ship is ready."

"What's going on here?" I asked.

Farr regarded me coldly. "I'm sending Erica and one of the weapons to New Chicago. Do you want to go as military escort?"

"New Chicago?" The more I thought about that, the less I liked it. "You mean you're going to put Erica and that damned bomb into a rocket plane and blast her halfway around Mars? The hell you are!"

"Garrett," Erica said. "Shut up."

"You shut up! I'm not letting you get in that stupid thing. What do they need a bomb for, anyway? What is all this—"

"Enough!" Farr shouted. "Lieutenant Pittson. The question is not whether Erica goes. That is settled, and you have no choice in the matter. The question is whether you will go, and frankly I don't think you're the proper man for the job, even if Erica has insisted that you come with her—"

"And just why isn't Garrett the right man?" Erica's voice was coldly polite.

"I think the two of you will drive me crazy," Farr said. "This is not only a technical job, it is also a diplomatic mission. You'll be working with university people, not Rimrats. Customs are different in the old colonies. And diplomacy is not precisely Garrett's strongest point."

"He'll be all right," Erica insisted. "And I want him with me. If—"

I didn't like the way she said that. "*If* what?" I asked.

Farr didn't answer immediately. He looked at Erica, then back to me, and finally came to a decision. "I see

I must explain. Garrett, that weapon must not fall into anyone else's hands. And we cannot allow the Federation to capture anyone who knows how many weapons we have. That is the main reason for the security we've put on the labs. What you don't know, you can't be forced to tell—and given modern interrogation methods, don't kid yourself that you won't tell everything you know. You will. It only takes time."

He looked at his left hand and tried to flex the fingers. "Fortunately, they did not have time in my case. And Mr. Ellsworth was less interested in information than in punishing a traitor. He is not a subtle man."

"Now wait a minute," I said. "You're saying that rather than be captured, we're supposed to commit suicide?"

"No. You don't know anything important. But Erica does. I believe the Padre preaches against suicide. . ."

"No! Goddamn it, are you telling me I have to kill Erica?"

"If that is the only alternative to capture, yes." He seemed pretty damn calm about it.

"I won't do it," I said.

"I supposed you would say that. So you will not be going. Someone else will."

"With the same orders," I said.

"Of course."

"That's inhuman!"

"Perhaps." Farr looked to Erica. She had shrunk down in her chair and looked miserable. "I told you," Farr said.

"Just wait," she said. She looked at me. "Please, Garrett? Nothing is going to happen. But if—well, I'd rather you were with me."

"But I love you," I told her. "Lord God, we fight a lot, but I do love you. How can you do this? Can't they send someone else?"

"Who?" Farr demanded.

"You will not send anyone else. Garrett, I have to do this. It's for the Project! Don't you see? I have to go."

I began to understand, then. "It's a lousy choice you're giving me."

"Nothing's going to happen," she said.

"If I thought this wouldn't work," Farr said, "I wouldn't risk it."

133

"The hell you wouldn't, I said. "You send women on suicide missions every day—"

"But I do not send out an irreplaceable weapon," Farr said. "I do not expect any trouble at all. But the military escort on this mission *must* understand the situation. Now, are you going or not?"

It was one hell of a choice, but not really. How could I stay behind, now that I knew what the orders were? I certainly couldn't stop her from going. I knew that. "All right, damn you, I'll go."

Before the Skipper opened his mouth I knew what the next thing would be. "Sarge tells me you're a Marsman," Farr said. "Are you?"

"Yes, sir."

"I have your word."

"Yes, sir."

"You'll leave in the morning. Under the circumstances, you're both off duty until then. I'll arrange for someone to put the gear you'll need aboard the ship."

15

When the dust is blowing, Mars' dawns are more brilliantly red than Earth's best sunsets. Thin clouds form streams of pink across the horizon, while overhead the stars shine with a luster you can never see on Earth. We watched the sunrise from the lip of a small crater about a hundred kilometers from Ice Hill. Farr's people had covered the crater with a nylon net; under it stood the rocket.

The bird stood on her tail inside the crater; when they rolled back the camouflage net, I saw that she was big, as big as a small airliner on Earth. I don't know why I'd expected something smaller. We didn't get a chance to see it very well because they hustled us down and inside and strapped us into seats.

There were eight of us as passengers. My own party, aside from Erica and myself, was Plemmons, who'd cut the monorail line back at Deucalion, and Doug, my communications man. In the forward seats were Dr. Weinbaum and two members of the Revolutionary Committee.

Weinbaum had been Chief Scientist for Mars Westinghouse. All the years he'd been with them he'd been part of the Mars freedom movement. I think some of the top brass at Westinghouse had suspected—the companies are perfectly capable of playing both sides of the street. Anyway, when the fighting broke out Weinbaum fled Marsport and eventually wound up at Ice Hill. I didn't know the other two. The three of them had big powwow to make with the Regents at New Chicago.

Their escort was Kehiayan, who'd been with me at Deucalion; this was like old home week. I didn't have to ask what his orders where if it looked like Weinbaum was going to be captured. They didn't give us much time for comradely reunion, and it was just as well; none of us were very cheerful. We remembered how many we'd left at Deucalion.

Once they got us strapped in they brought in a box about a meter long and half that in cross section, and strapped it into the seat next to Erica. Nobody mentioned it. I looked at it and shuddered. Okay, it's a silly reaction; but after all, the Federation was formed to keep Earth safe from nuclear wars, and every teacher in school had pounded in the lesson that there was nothing more horrible than an atom bomb. You don't easily get over that kind of indoctrination.

There wasn't any ceremony. First there was the noise of the engines, and then we felt weight. The ship accelerated slowly at first, then picked up until I suppose we were at two or three Earth gravities. That was no strain on me, but for Erica and the others born on Mars it was seven times what they were used to, and it must have been torture.

After a couple of minutes the engines cut. It was dead quiet in the cabin. With the low pressure you couldn't even hear whispers. Dr. Weinbaum took a pipe out of his pocket and tried to lay it down on the ashtray. It floated up and drifted away in a random air current. We were in free fall.

Erica let go the straps and shoved herself away from the chair. She pushed too hard and bounced off the ceiling, swam helplessly for a moment, and laughed. We all did. None of us had ever had a chance to play in free fall before. My one experience, coming down from the prison ship in the landing boat, didn't help; when I let go I pushed too hard and followed almost the same route Erica had. Eventually we swam over to the view port.

We were crossing from daylight into darkness. Mars looked cut in half, the dark portion only visible because it blocked out the stars. At the edge of the planet you could see the atmosphere, incredibly thin, a tiny thing. I pointed to it.

"There will be more," Erica said. "If this works. And I know it will." Her voice took on that glowing quality they all had when they talked about the Project. I didn't respond.

Directly below us was one of the famous wandering canyons that drive scientists crazy. If you saw it on Earth you'd *know* it was a dry riverbed. There are a lot of them on Mars, and they *must* have been cut by water, but nobody knows for sure where the water went—or where it came from. Right next to the canyon was a big crater, half a million years old, with no trace of water erosion.

Dr. Weinbaum was discussing it with his colleagues. "It certainly didn't *rain*," he said. "So how does water cut a canyon as deep as any on Earth, and leave an enormous crater standing next to it untouched?"

Our trajectory carried us northwest, and we passed over the east edge of Coprates, the Grand Canyon of Mars. If the other canyons irritate the scientists, this one gives them the screaming willies. It's longer than the United States is wide, and four miles deep in places. The walls are steep cliffs as high as Earth's biggest mountains. The canyon is closed at both ends, so it certainly wasn't formed by water —but no one knows where all the cubic miles of material that used to be in there have gone.

We could just make out the monorail running from the east edge of Coprates to Novoya Sverdlovsk in Edom. There are several big mining colonies in the canyon, and the monorail stops there. The Federation had been talking about extending it westward another two thousand miles to the university colonies, but they hadn't done it. It would be a hell of a big project.

After that we were over the nightside, and we went back to our seats. I took Erica's hand, and she smiled softly, then went to sleep. I leaned back, and the pistol on my belt dug into my ribs. It reminded me of my orders, and once again I shuddered.

As planned, we landed in darkness, in a crater forty kilometers from New Chicago. The Free Mars movement at New Chicago was supposed to send a party to meet us.

Unless the universities came over to the independence movement, we were probably there for keeps. There aren't very many independent stations near the university colonies, probably not enough to manufacture the fuel the rocket plane would need to take us home. The universities could do it, but only if they took control away from the Feddies. I wished Weinbaum well; this didn't look like a good place to try to set up a station. It was late fall in the northern hemisphere, and although we were reasonably close to the equator, it was cold outside. I went out first.

Tractors bathed us in light. Three figures got out of one tractor and came toward the plane. I held my submachine gun tightly. They came closer and raised their hands to show they were empty. A female voice came into my headset. "Listen my children, and you shall hear," she said.

"Of slithy toves, that gyre and gimbel in the slot machine," I answered.

"For all is vanity," she said. "Mars and Freedom. Welcome to New Chicago."

I relaxed. There were a dozen possible variations in those code words, but she'd given none of the warning signals. Her welcome to New Chicago was a bit premature: we were a long way from the universities, and Erica and I weren't going there. I went back in for the others. Plemmons, Doug, and Kehiayan were waiting near the hatch, weapons ready. Erica and the Committee people were clustered at the opposite end. They looked scared. "All's well," I told them.

Weinbaum and his colleagues got into one tractor, which drove away quickly. They wanted to be inside the university before dawn. There were three more tractors for my party. Erica insisted that we put the bomb in the cabin with her; she wasn't going to let it out of her sight. Doug and I got in with her, and I put Plemmons in another tractor behind us. All the tractors pulled power-unit trailers, and there was a lot of other gear loaded on them.

As soon as we were loaded we drove out of the crater. "My name's Eileen," our driver said. "Hi."

We introduced ourselves. She had heard about the big Deucalion raid. "That must have been exciting," she said. "It took a lot of guts."

"Mostly just hard work," I said, but I was flattered just the same.

There wasn't enough light to see much, but the terrain seemed to open up once we got out of the crater where the rocket plane was hidden. Eileen drove without maps, just following the compass; in a few minutes I was lost. I couldn't see her very well. She had her helmet on, faceplate open. In the dark that didn't show a lot, but she had a nice voice.

Erica didn't say anything, and after a while I told her, "Sweetheart, you've had it. Why don't you climb into the back and get some sleep? You'll have that damn bomb for a bunkmate, but I guess you've shared beds with worse."

"All right. I am tired." She climbed out of the seat, and in five minutes she was out. Doug curled up in his seat and began snoring gently.

"Wide-awake troops," Eileen said. There was a laugh in her voice.

"Been a long month," I said. "Doug's been on the perimeter patrol since Deucalion."

"I'm sorry. I didn't mean anything." We drove on through the night.

Dawn came about two hours later. First there was a faint pink tinge in the east, nothing like the spectacular dawn we had left behind, then the edge of the sun showed and we had full light. I looked at the landscape around us. It was not like the southern hemisphere. We were in a huge plain. There were very few rocks and craters and no hills at all. Just a flat plain, not much dust blowing, with isolated high mountains thrusting upward at random intervals. The mountains seemed enormous.

"Volcanoes," Eileen told me. "You don't have any in the south."

"No."

"What do you do when you're not fighting wars?" Eileen asked.

"Rimrat," I said. "Station owner. Make that apprentice station owner. I'd have my own except for the war, but it's not in yet. You?"

"Student. Mining engineering. My father's on the faculty Council, Dr. Hermans."

I'd never heard of him, but I supposed he was one of

the people Weinbaum was meeting. "Erica's an engineer," I said.

"Oh? What school?"

I laughed at that. "TV screen. Hellastown library. She's a Rimrat. Her father's got one of the most successful operations on the Rim. We don't have schools."

"Oh. Is she your roommate?"

Now what the hell kind of question is that? I wondered. I remembered Farr's little talk about customs being different in the north. "We're engaged. My sponsor was negotiating with her father when the war started."

"That sounds like a business deal."

"Well, it's necessary." I tried to explain about Rim customs. "What's it like in New Chicago?"

She told me, but I didn't really understand. It was too unfamiliar. The university ran the town and owned most of it. There were labor clients, and a few transportees, but they didn't really count. Neither did the independent station owners. Eileen either didn't know or didn't care how they lived or what their customs were.

In the cities the university families tended to marry late, or set up housekeeping without marrying at all. Either way it was no big deal and there were few formalities. "Except for the religious types," she said. Children were raised by either parent, or by the university school system. A few students came up from Earth, but most were from Marsport and other "civilian" communities. That was her word, not mine. Faculty children tended to stay and become faculty members themselves; outsiders usually took their degrees and went back where they'd come from.

I told her about life on the Rim. It was almost an alien experience to her. She wanted to know how I'd gotten into the war, and I told her about the boycott because of Federation taxes. "I hadn't really thought about war," I said. "Independence was something we talked about in gatherings, but it was always going to happen a long time off. Then all of a sudden we were in the middle of it. How did you get involved with Free Mars?"

"Well, I told you my father's on the faculty Council. He's been corresponding with Dr. Weinbaum for years. So naturally I'm involved. We're not firebrand revolutionaries, Garrett. The Federation has treated us pretty well. But that doesn't mean we don't care. The whole labor client system is nothing more than slavery. We have to care." She was quiet for a moment. "What's going to happen after you people take control of Mars?"

I laughed. "We've got to do it first. Me, I'll go back and set up my station. The Skipper says I've got that coming. When the war's over, all the Rimrats will get together and rebuild Windhome, and the other ruined places, and help Erica and me get our station in. Won't be much different from the way things have always been on the Rim, except we won't have tax collectors to break our backs."

"Yes, but there's got to be some government," she said. "You can't throw out the Federation and not replace it."

"Yeah, but it's not my problem. I can leave that to the big brains."

"But what happens if you don't *like* what your revolutionary committee puts together?" she asked.

"Then I guess we'll just have to throw them out as well. What can they do? Collect taxes on the Rim again? Who with? What for? Why shouldn't we like what our own committee sets up?"

"You don't know much history, do you, Garrett?" she asked.

"No. What's that got to do with it?"

"Forget it. Tell me about the Deucalion raid. Did you kill many people? What's it like to be in a battle?"

"You don't think much about it at the time," I told her. "You just do it. The thinking comes later." Or before. Especially before. "I suppose you'll have your share of fighting here. If Weinbaum and your father can bring it off—"

"Not as much as you'd think. There aren't but a few hundred Federation people here, and some of them are university police who'll do what the faculty Council tells them. We won't have much fighting, except for the power plants."

Something about the way she said that bothered me. She must have sensed it, because she said, "We're a backwater, Gary. I suppose we're important to Mars, but as schools and scientists. How can the Federation force us to do anything? Can they force us to teach? So they leave us pretty well alone."

That wasn't what had bothered me. If they could heave the Feddies out without fighting, why hadn't they done it?

Why were we hiding our ship out in a crater instead of bringing it into the New Chicago landing field? Didn't these people *care?*

I told myself it wasn't my problem. There was nothing I could do, anyway. Weinbaum would have to take care of that.

"Tell me more about the battles," she said. "Tell me what it's like."

We made camp out on the sands that night. The university people had brought plenty of gear, including a big pressure tent that would hold all of us. We met the others at dinner. There were about a dozen university people. The man in charge was Dr. Drury, a junior member of the engineering faculty at New Chicago. He explained that he was really a geophysicist, but he taught engineering, and he liked fieldwork.

There wasn't a lot of conversation. We were all tired from bouncing around in the tractors since before dawn. The food was good, and there were three cooks who served it and cleaned up afterward. We weren't introduced to them.

Drury was a strange one. He kept talking to Erica about the bomb. It was obvious that he knew more about making them than she did, but the Federation had never let the universities have any refined uranium. The power plant was staffed by Federation people and guarded by marines, and the faculty weren't admitted.

"It's a breeder pile," Drury said. "They aren't getting anything like the efficiency they ought to. But they operate it themselves and take all the uranium back to that depository in Deucalion, then ship it back to Earth. Won't let us help them at all. Stupid."

"Garrett was in charge of the force that captured Deucalion," Eileen said.

"Oh? Good work," Drury said. He turned back to Erica, and asked her about implosion lenses. I think that's what he said.

I didn't think she was enjoying the conversation. "Guess it's about time to turn in," I said. "Don, you want the first watch?"

"Suits," Plemmons said.

"Thanks. Dr. Drury, if you'll show us where we sleep—"

Eileen looked confused. "You don't have to keep watches. We've got people to do that."

"Sorry," I said. "Orders. We watch that bomb until it goes off."

"I'll take a watch," Erica said.

"No. No need. We've got nothing else to do, but you've got brain work. Get some sleep."

They'd set up two separate pressure tents for our group and put my gear in with Erica's. I didn't like the arrangements. She wouldn't let the bomb out of her sight, and we had to keep watches. I wasn't about to have anyone —including me—sit outside at night. I made them move the four of us, and the bomb, into one tent, where one of us could sit up on watch. We slept in our p-suits and helmets anyway. The university people laughed at us for that. They had double-walled tents and weren't afraid of blowouts.

"Yeah, but what if the Feddies find out where we are?" I asked.

"They won't," Eileen said. "And they'd never get here without someone knowing they were coming. I keep telling you, my father's on the faculty Council."

I didn't understand what the hell that had to do with anything. But I hadn't missed that she said "you people" when she referred to the Free Mars movement. Maybe it wasn't the Feddies we had to worry about.

I got Erica tucked in, and Doug climbed into his sleeping bag to catch some rest. Don Plemmons and I had a few words before he took first watch.

"I don't like these people, Garrett," he said. "They treat me like dirt. They give orders like Feddies, and they don't even wait to find out if you've got something else to do."

"They've been all right to me," I said.

"You're an officer."

"What the hell difference does that make?" I asked.

"It does. Watch and see. These people aren't Marsmen, Garrett. Not Marsmen at all."

"Crap. They've been here longer than we have. Third and fourth generation."

"Yeah. But they aren't Marsmen."

"Don't be stupid. I'll relieve you in three hours," I said. "No point in trying to sleep for that short a time. I'll stay up. Maybe I can find some company in the university tent."

"Okay, chief." He crawled into our tent. I'd rather have sat up with him, but Erica and Doug couldn't have got any sleep with us chattering.

Drury and Eileen were in the command tent. They acted glad to see me when I came in.

"Eileen has been telling me about your experiences at Deucalion," Drury said. "Maybe you can help us."

"How?"

"Well, we are going to have to storm that power plant," Drury said. "And we've never—well, maybe you could help. Command the assault force when the time comes. After all, you've got experience in that line."

"I do now. But only because we had a job to do and we did it. I'm sure your people—I mean, you've got to do it yourselves, you know. We can't take that power plant for you."

Drury looked serious. "I know that. People will be killed. I'm glad I don't have to decide who it will be. Perhaps we can persuade the Federation to give up without a fight."

"Could be." I didn't really believe it.

"Do you want a drink?" Drury asked.

"I've got guard duty coming up. I better pass."

"How about coffee?" Eileen asked.

"Coffee? Sure. We don't have any coffee on the Rim. Haven't had any since I left Earth."

"It's about time, then," Eileen said. "Joseph, some coffee for Lieutenant Pittson, please."

I hadn't seen the other man. He was sitting in the back of the tent, near the kitchen area. One of the cooks. He brought a ceramic mug and handed it to me. It smelled great. I held it to my nose and sniffed it, savoring it. "Thank you," I said. I meant it.

"You're welcome," Drury said.

I hadn't spoken to him. I'd said my thanks to Joseph, who'd brought it, but the cook had gone back to his seat in the back of the tent. I wondered about him. Labor client? Did the universities have labor clients? Why the hell would a man be a servant?

Drury had a nightcap, and excused himself. "We'll be there at noon tomorrow," he said. "Work to do. I'd better turn in. Eileen, will you be needing anything else from the kitchen?"

"I can manage," she said.

"All right. Joseph, you can go to bed now."

"Thank you, Doctor. Good night." They left together.

"More coffee?" Eileen asked.

"Sure. Thanks. How do you grow this, anyway?"

"I'm afraid I don't know," she said. "We've always had coffee at the university. You can ask the agriculture people when you meet them."

"Yeah, I'll have to." If I could grow coffee, I could get a good price for it. Or could I? Would the Rimrats have got out of the habit? Nobody born on Mars had ever tasted the stuff. Hell, if there wasn't a market I'd make one—Mars and coffee were made for each other It would be worth it, though, just to have some for myself.

"What's with Joseph?" I asked. "Is he a labor client?"

"Good heavens no." She was shocked. "He's a university cook. Part of the staff. Labor client!" She laughed then. "There are fifty people who'd like to have his job." She moved over closer, almost touching me. They'd brought inflatable plastic couches.

She was a very pretty girl. Short, with dark hair and brown eyes, her hair cut short also, with a red ribbon in it. Erica had been busy the last two weeks, and I found myself having disturbing thoughts. Eileen seemed to like me, too.

Don't be a damn fool, Garrett, I told myself. You've got nothing in common with this girl. So what? myself retorted.

"I think everyone else has gone to bed," Eileen said. She leaned against me. I could feel her warmth. There was no mistaking the invitation.

"Guess I'd better have a look around the perimeter," I said.

"Why? You're not on guard for two hours. What's wrong with you?" She reached out and pulled me toward her. "I know damned well I turn you on."

"Yeah, you do. But I told you, I'm engaged—"

"What on Mars does that have to do with anything?" she asked.

"Erica is probably the most monogamous woman who ever lived," I said. "Look, I'd love to hop in the sack with you, but nothing good can come of it—"

"You people are all crazy," she spat. "Possessive relationships. Bride prices—that's what it is, isn't it? Bride price and dowry. Sexual repressions. You're primitives. Probably that's why you like fighting and wars."

"What the hell's got you mad? And we don't *like* wars. It's just that we won't be pushed around. I told you how I got into this—"

"You sure did. It sounded to me like you liked it. And you fight duels. With knives."

"Yeah, sometimes. But it's no big thing. Look, I'd better go."

"Go on. But you can't say you don't want me. And you can't tell me how it would hurt your precious Ice Queen—"

"Now what the hell are you talking about?"

Eileen laughed. "I've seen the way she treats you. Cold. Expects you to do things for her. If you two are in love, I'm a purple sand cat. But she owns you—"

"Bullshit. She's got the responsibility for that damned bomb, and she's worried about whether it will work, and—"

"Sure," Eileen said. "Sure. Just go on, now. Go prowl around the desert looking for Federation police! There aren't any for two hundred kilometers, I told you that, but you just go play soldier. I'm out of the mood, anyway."

There are times when I think women are a separate species entirely.

16

The volcano rose above a series of rocky plateaus piled on each other like poker chips of decreasing sizes stacked into a cone. The mountain jutted more than a mile above the topmost plate. On Earth it would have been an enormous mountain, but it was small for Mars.

We reached it at noon the next day. A large permanent camp had been set up at its base, and a big drilling rig was already in operation. The derrick was dwarfed by the mountain rising into the dark sky behind it.

The drill crew was mostly made up of independent station owners. The crew chief called himself Tex, and had worked for an oil outfit on Earth before he killed a man in a fight and ended up sentenced to transportation for life. He'd been sent as a labor client to work in one of the mine camps in East Coprates.

"Hard work," he told us. "Wind whistles through that damn big ditch. Not much sun down there. Coldern' Pluto's balls. And they worked us like slaves. Never anything to spend money on, no place to go, guards beatin' on your head all the time. Got sick of it. So one morning some of the gang and me stole two tractors and came here."

147

"You came three thousand kilometers in tractors?" Don Plemmons asked.

"Yep."

"How?"

"With great difficulty," Cal said. Cal was a black miner who'd come out with Tex. "Started with twenty men, got here with nine. Took up with some farmers. Did all right."

"Are most of the station owners here for Free Mars?"

"Yeah, most of 'em," Cal said.

"How do you get along with the university people?" Plemmons asked.

Tex shrugged. "Mostly we don't have much to do with 'em. The word came out that the bigdomes wanted a hole drilled. The Project, they said. So here we are. Kind of snooty lot, seems to us. Don't ever have much to say. I don't think they like convicts."

"They're on our side," I said. "These are, anyway."

"Yeah, reckon so," Tex said. "Much as they're on anybody's side. Except their own."

They were drilling a slant hole from the base of the mountain down under the crater floor. It was a big operation. In addition to the drilling rig, they had to mine ice for water. The drill wouldn't work without a lot of water pumped down the hole.

The drill was fascinating. A big derrick held pipes vertical, and electric motors run by solar cells turned them. Every few minutes the crew would connect another piece of pipe to the one vanishing into the ground. "The drill string's following a kind of soft area in the rock," Tex told us. "We're about two kilometers in already." The pipes turned endlessly, while a stream of dirty water bubbled out of the hole to run off into the sands and vanish a few feet away. Even at this cold temperature it boiled in the thin air of Mars.

We called GHQ at Ice Hill, relaying through the captured ship in orbit above Mars. "It looks pretty good," Erica told Commander Farr. "They've got the hole mostly drilled already."

"How's the cooperation with the university people?" Farr asked.

"It couldn't be better," Erica said. "Dr. Drury's a Project fanatic. And they have this huge effort, drillers, miles of pipe, everything. They're really splendid."

"I'm glad to hear that," Farr said. "Weinbaum isn't getting anywhere in the negotiations. Everything has to be referred to three different committees, and the people who have to make decisions can't be reached—I guess it's just their way. I don't mind telling you I was getting worried, but if your part's going all right, it doesn't matter."

"Doesn't matter?" I took the mike. "Skipper, if they don't get together on this, we can't get home! No fuel for the rocket plane."

"We'll get you home," Farr said. "You just see this thing goes off properly. We're counting on you. When that bomb goes off it'll be the signal for the general uprising in the cities. It will show everyone on Earth that we can make atomic weapons, and it will show the miners and townspeople that we're serious about the Project. It *must* work, and it must work on time."

"It will," Erica said. "The bomb will work, and I've been over the plan with Dr. Drury. The plug stopping up the volcano is nothing but some hardened granite. The bomb will crack it, and the pressure underneath will do the rest. It will work."

"I'm damned glad you're so sure of it," Farr said. "Because we'll have to surface a lot of our agents just before it goes. If we broadcast an appeal and nothing happens, it will set us back months. Not to mention getting a lot of good people killed. If this thing won't go, let me know before it's too late."

"The odds haven't changed," Erica said. Her voice was cold and distant. "You knew the risks when you decided to do this."

"Yes. There are always risks. This one seems the best chance of ending this war quickly. We'll go with the plan," Farr said. "GHQ out."

"We'll go with the plan," Erica said to me. "And I won't be able to rest until this thing is done. Poor Garrett, I haven't been very nice to be around, have I? I'm sorry, darling."

"It's all right," I said.

"No, it's not. But I can't help it." She came to me and

149

we stood, embracing. "I'm glad you're here, even if you weren't needed," she said.

"That's a hell of a way to put it—"

"Oh, Garrett, I didn't want it that way. But you weren't needed, were you? We're perfectly safe here. The university people couldn't treat us any better."

"Yeah—"

"You sound suspicious," Erica said. "Why?"

"No good reason," I told her. "It's just that this is such a damned big operation. Drillers, miles of pipe, the rig, an acre of solar cells spread out on the mountain side, tractors, permanent buildings—it's too much. They couldn't have kept this hidden from the Feddies."

"But they did. We haven't been bothered."

"Yeah. All the same, I'll be glad to get back home." I pulled her to me and kissed her. Then again. Then—

"Not now," she said impatiently. "Please. I want to check some figures—"

"I sort of had figure checking in mind myself," I said. I looked at her to show what figure I had in mind.

"I have to work. And we've got to make an early start in the morning. Dr. Drury is taking us to the top of the volcano. I want to get some sleep." She pulled away. "Good night, Garrett. I love you."

"Yeah. Sure. I love you to—"

She went into her room and closed the door. They'd given us a concrete blockhouse, with an air-lock, and a big main room, and three smaller rooms. There was even running water, hot water in the daytime. I had the bomb put in one of the rooms, and one of my troops was awake and in the blockhouse at all times. Erica thought I was silly; when we first came she wouldn't let it out of her sight, but now she said I was making a fool of myself, and insulting our hosts as well, by insisting on guarding it with our own people rather than let the university staff take care of it.

I thought she was probably right, but the Skipper had made it clear that the damn thing was *ours*, and we would set it off at the right time and place. I went over to the desk and sat down to take the first watch.

It's soft duty, I told myself. And there's coffee to drink. Relax and enjoy it.

Drury had instruments set up all around the area. Every now and then he'd blow off a dynamite charge and needles would squiggle as the shock waves passed. By feeding the squiggles into a computer he got a picture of the rock and gunk under the volcano. The bomb had to be placed just right so it would crack the rocks that plugged up the lava and gas flow. If everything went right when we blew the weapon, there would be a big gusher of water vapor and gas.

We drove up the side of the mountain the next day. I left Doug and Don Plemmons sitting on the bomb so I could stay with Erica. It took most of the morning to drive up the side of the big mountain, even though the university had blasted out a road years before.

"This one volcano won't do much," Drury told us as we drove up. "But if—no, when—this works we'll have others. I'll show you, up on the rim."

When we reached the top we got out and looked over the edge. The volcano floor was far below. It was flat and smooth. "This was active not a thousand years ago," Drury said. "An instant, geologically speaking. It's still got plenty of pressure underneath. A single bomb should do it. But come look here."

He led the way up a series of steps cut into a big rock at the rim edge. There was a flat place on top where you had a view of the plains all around us. "Look out there," Drury said. He pointed northeast. "We're standing on a little baby, but look at that."

He was pointing to an enormous, cone-shaped mountain. Its base was beyond the horizon, over a hundred miles away, but still it was huge, like Manhattan Island standing on end, ten miles high. "When we set *that* off, you'll know it! And it's not the biggest we have, either." He pointed northwest. "You can't see it, but over that way is Olympus Mons, the granddaddy of them all. Biggest mountain in the solar system. Fifteen miles high, higher than from the bottom of the deepest sea on Earth to the top of Mount Everest. They could see it from Earth before the spacecraft ever got here. Nix Olympica, they called it. Snows of Olympus. You can see the cloud cover over it."

There were thin white clouds out where he pointed.

"One day we'll wake him up," Drury said. "That will really be something to see."

I still made rounds at night. It seemed silly and I knew it, but I couldn't get over the feeling that an operation this big couldn't be hidden. The Federation still controlled everything in this part of Mars. Even the station owners were careful to hide their revolutionary sympathies. And there might not be very many Feddie cops out here, but there were enough to roll over us.

I couldn't help thinking how safe the people at Deucalion had thought they were. So every evening I went out and made rounds, just before sundown, and then later, in the dark, watched for any signs of movement out on the plains. I never saw anything, of course.

I made night rounds and went into the cook shack to find some coffee. I got a cup. The place was deserted, so I sprawled out and relaxed. Then Eileen came in and took off her helmet.

"I wasn't very nice to you the other night," she said. "I'm sorry—"

"It's okay."

"Sure." She got herself a cup and sat next to me. "Ice Princess all bedded down?"

"I wish you wouldn't talk about Erica that way."

"Sorry, but she is and you know it. She have a headache or what?"

"Eileen, for heaven's sake—"

"What are you so nervous about?" she asked. "Look. We're adults, we're the same age, and we turn each other on. Why shouldn't we do something about it? Like this." She leaned toward me and kissed me.

We set the coffee cups down and tried that again. After a while she reached for the tab on the big spiral zipper on my pressure suit.

"Maybe we better open the inner door to the air lock," I said.

"I already left it open."

There wasn't any conversation for a long time after that.

I didn't like myself very much the next day. I kept telling myself there was no harm done. Erica hadn't lost anything. I still loved her. She had no use for me. Nothing was changed between us. And the rest of it. Every man has his own set of excuses, and mine weren't very original.

The work went on. Erica and Drury worked every day, getting the drill string sent down just right, making certain the bomb would fit in the drill casing and go smoothly to the proper place. The drill could only work when the sun was up, of course; there weren't enough batteries and fuel cells to power it at night. But from before dawn to that last bit of sun, the crew was working, and so was Erica.

It left me a lot of time with Eileen. She'd look me up, "just to keep me company," she said, and sit with me on guard watches. When I was on watch we just talked. She'd never been to Earth, of course, and I found myself telling her a lot of things I'd told Erica. Eileen was a good listener.

Then came the day: the hole was finished. Erica lowered the bomb into the shaft. It took all day and part of the night to get it placed right. Then the drill crew pumped mud in on top of it to seal in the blast.

"It's topped up," Tex said. "Our job's done."

Erica brought in her detonator. It was built into a radio chassis. "I suppose there ought to be some kind of ceremony," she said. "Here goes." She threw two switches, and three lights glowed on the box.

"It's armed," Erica said. A broad grin broke out on her face. "It really works! Nothing can stop it now. Let's tell the Skipper!"

It took an hour to set up the relay link. Erica told Commander Farr what we'd done.

"And you're sure everything is set?" Farr demanded.

"Yes, sir," Erica told him. "The responder worked, and that shows we have communications with the device. Now it will detonate when I send the right signal. The bomb can't be disarmed unless you know the proper frequencies and codes, and I've allowed no one to examine the detonator. I didn't even choose the final frequencies until this morning."

"And you've got the detonator under guard?" Farr said.

"Certainly."

There was a long pause on the other end. Then Farr

said, "Okay. We'll go with the plan. I want that thing to go off exactly at thirteen hundred Mars Zulu the day after tomorrow. That's 5:00 A.M. your time. Not tomorrow, the day after, at 5:00 A.M. your time. Understood?"

"Yes, sir," Erica said.

"Good. That will be late afternoon at Marsport. We'll start broadcasting the message four hours before Go. An hour later we'll have to reveal your location. You run like hell as soon as she goes. That okay with you?"

"Yes." Erica said.

"All right," Farr said. "There's a lot riding on this. The big uprisings will come when the ship gets telephotos of that volcano going up and broadcasts them all over Mars. We're telling the miners and the other labor clients that the Project will be the first thing Free Mars will do. We're telling them their kids will be able to go take free land and live on it without all the expensive equipment they'd need to set up stations. And we're telling Earth to look close, because this could be what happens to your city if the Federation ever bombs one of ours."

"The big push is set for when we detonate the bomb?" I asked.

"Yes. Make sure it's on time. A lot of our people will have to surface, and if that thing doesn't go on time, we'll lose them."

"I understand," I said. "We'll sit guard on the detonator until it's time. How's Weinbaum doing with the negotiations?"

"Still delays. He thinks the Regents are waiting to see which way the wind blows. They'll come over if there's a general uprising, and if Earth doesn't look like bombing us out. Your little stunt ought to convince them. But you've got your secondary contacts just in case, right?"

"Yes, sir," I said. We'd been given the names and locations of some friendly station owners who'd hide us if the university people couldn't take care of us.

"All's well, then," Farr said. "This is it. In a couple of hundred hours it should be all over except for mopping up. GHQ out."

We carried the detonator into our blockhouse. Erica put it in her room.

"It seems too good to be true," I told her. "The war over—"

"Maybe," Erica said. She looked at the box with its glowing lights. "Anyway, my job's done. Nothing left to do but push a button at the right time. Until then, there's nothing I *can* do. It's over."

"Over for us." I thought about my buddies back at the Rim. Sarge would be leading an attack on Hellastown. I wondered how many would be killed.

"Garrett, I don't know how you've stood up to all this," Erica said. "I'm exhausted." She came over and put her arms around me. I held her close. We kissed, then again.

"I thought you were exhausted," I said.

"Not *that* exhausted. Who's outside?"

"Don's in the main room—"

"Close the door. Then come here."

For a moment I thought about Eileen and I felt like a bloody heel, but then I wasn't thinking about anything at all.

17

We got our gear packed up and ready so we could run. After that there was nothing to do but wait. Erica and I stayed in the blockhouse. We had decided we wouldn't leave until the bomb went off. Later, Dr. Drury came in to have supper with us, while Doug sat in Erica's room with the detonator.

"It will be a magnificent thing," Drury said. "Magnificent. Making over a whole world. We can all be proud to have been part of it."

"It will take a long time," Erica said.

Drury nodded. "But we can speed it up. Melt off the polar caps—"

"They melt every summer anyway," I said.

"Not all of them. One melts, the other forms. But there are ways to keep them melted. And there are layers of both poles that never melt at all. We've studied this extensively. The Project can be speeded up enormously— and will be, when the Federation gets out of the way."

"I'm glad we've got you people on our side," Erica said. She waved at the blockhouse. "This would be a building to be proud of back home. Here it's just a temporary thing at a research camp. You've got enormous capabilities at the university."

"Thank you," Drury said. He raised his glass. "To the Project!"

We all drank to that.

"Of course," Drury said, "not everybody at New Chicago U is a Project enthusiast—"

"I'd have thought they would be," I said.

"Well, some think we don't understand Mars yet. They want to study it the way it is. They have a point; there's a lot to learn, a lot we can learn about Earth by studying Mars. We'll lose most of that information when the atmosphere begins to build up."

"How long do they want to wait?" Erica asked.

Drury shrugged. "They don't say. But have you ever heard of a research project being *finished?*"

We laughed at that. I had two glasses of wine, then switched to coffee. "I still won't feel right until that damn thing's set off and we see the gusher," I said.

The party broke up about eleven. Drury went to his quarters and I got a nap. I relieved Doug about 2:00 A.M.

"One day and night after this," I said. "Get some sleep. I'll catch Plemmons for the next watch."

"Right."

I made sure the inner door of the air-lock was open. I was wearing my suit, and had my helmet beside me. With that air-lock door open nobody could get in without blowing out the blockhouse, and we could still trigger the bomb. It would go off early and spoil the Skipper's big speech, but it would still show Earth we knew how to make nukes—and show Mars that we were serious about the Project, too.

The Project was the big thing with the labor clients. All our agents told us that. With the Project under way there was hope for anybody. A lot of workers would probably choose to stay with the big companies. We were telling Mars' industries that if they didn't help the Federation against us, we'd let them keep everything they had except labor contracts; if they could hire workers, and they probably could, they could go on mining, refining, selling to Earth, and making big profits.

Actually we were going to need the companies. If they closed down there'd be no employment for most of our people.

I'd been sitting in the main room, thinking about what

I'd do with my valley and wondering if I could get coffee beans to grow. After about an hour the air-lock speaker was activated.

"Garrett?"

Eileen. I didn't want to see her. I felt ashamed of myself for ever getting involved with her.

"I couldn't sleep," she said. "Let me in."

Oh hell, I thought. I couldn't argue with her while she stood out in the cold, and I did owe her something—I could hardly tell a girl I'd been sleeping with to get lost. I closed the inner air-lock door and waited for the lock to cycle.

"Cold out there," she said. "Hi."

"Hi yourself."

She sat down on the other side of the room. "It's a long night."

"Yeah. Tomorrow will be longer."

"This one's long enough." She bounced up. "I'm restless. Got any coffee?"

"Sure."

"Here, I'll get yours too." She took my cup and filled it and one for herself. "Everybody asleep?"

"Yeah. If you're going to drink that, you'd better take your helmet off. It dribbles inside if you try to drink through the faceplate. Or it does for me."

"In a minute. I almost froze out there." She sipped at the cup. As I'd warned, she spilled some inside her helmet. "That's good. Aren't you having any?"

"In a minute. I'm about coffeed out."

"I guess I will take off this helmet. Give me a hand?"

"Sure." I went over to help with the thing. As I got to her, she raised a little cylinder, about the size of a lipstick, and a small cloud of spray came out into my face.

"Wha—" I tried to shout, but I couldn't. My face was paralyzed. My vision began to go, not so much dark as that nothing made sense. I vaguely saw that she'd slammed down her faceplate and was sealed up.

I couldn't do anything. I gradually felt my knees giving away and knew I was falling, but I couldn't do anything about that, either. I tried to get a deep breath but nothing happened, and now things began to get darker and darker, and she was going back into the blockhouse toward Erica's room and there was nothing I could do about it, nothing at all.

I thought I was back in Baltimore Undertown, because I heard sirens and gunshots, and I tried to fight the Hackers who'd jumped me but I couldn't move. Then I passed out.

"Garrett! Garrett, O God let him be all right! Garrett!"

Someone was shouting in my ear. Part of my mind knew it was Erica and wanted to answer, but I couldn't answer because I couldn't control my lungs. I felt my chest expand and contract. It was a curious feeling, because I hadn't told it to do that.

I opened my eyes. They wouldn't focus on anything. There was a big white blur above me. The blur had blue eyes and red hair. It moved away and there was another blur that looked like Doug, only his face was clearer, and after a moment things swam into shape.

Doug was bending over me holding an oxygen mask over my mouth and nose. He was manipulating an oxygen bottle to force air into my lungs, then he'd turn it off and shove hard on my chest. He kept doing that.

Don Plemmons held guard on the airlock with an automatic rifle. The inner door was open. On the other side of the room Eileen stood flattened against the wall, as Erica alternately slapped her and shook her.

"What have you done to him?" Slap. "Tell us!" Shake. "If he dies, I'll—" It went on like that.

She said some horrible things. I don't remember most of them. I don't *want* to remember them. I didn't know Erica knew that much physiology.

Eileen was white with fear. She tried to talk, but Erica kept slapping her. Finally Erica let her alone. "I don't know what it was," Eileen sobbed. "It was some kind of gas, they told me it wouldn't kill anyone, just paralyze him. I don't know!"

"Nerve gas," Doug said. "Don, there's stuff for that in the med kit. Get 'em and a hypo."

Don vanished. I couldn't turn my head to see where he went, but after a while he was back again.

I felt a stabbing pain in my thigh. Then another in my neck. "Maybe that'll do it," Doug said. "It's supposed to be a remedy. All we got, anyway." He kept on working with the mask. "Can you hear us, Garrett?" he asked.

"Awugll." I was surprised that I could say anything at all.

"Maybe he'll make it," Doug said. "Erica, if she don't know, she don't know. You can stop shaking her."

"Yes." She came back over to me and knelt beside me. "Please be all right, Garrett. Please."

"Urk." Something was happening. I tried to help the breathing process. After about three tries I was able to inhale. Then exhale.

"What the hell do we do now?" Plemmons said.

"Watch that damn box," Doug said. "Stay close to it and trigger the bomb if it looks like we've had it. But wait as long as we can."

"Maybe we ought to set it off now," Don Plemmons said.

"Think we should wait," Doug said. "Erica? It's your baby."

"We wait. How is he?"

"Tryin' to breathe," Doug said. "I think he is going to make it. Maybe we ought to shoot that bitch now and get it over with?"

"No," I managed to say.

"So you can talk," Erica said.

I got in a deep breath. "Need to find out why," I said. "How many in on this."

"Good thinking," Plemmons said. "Lady, unless you like breathin' Mars air without a helmet, you better tell us what this is all about."

Eileen was crying.

"I can't believe Dr. Drury knew," Erica said. "He's all for the Project."

"No Marsman," Plemmons said. "He don't give shit about Free Mars."

"No, but he is for the Project," Erica insisted.

"Drillers," I managed to say. "Drillers are patriots. Get help."

"He's right," Plemmons said.

"Sure, and how many of this chick's friends are out there waitin' for her to get through killin' us all in our beds?" Doug asked. "Go out that air lock, and maybe you face a couple dozen Feddie cops."

"We've got to do something," Erica said.

"First thing is we beat shit out of that chick," Plemmons said. "She'll talk."

"No," I said. "We don't work that way." I took a deep breath. Then another. I flexed my fingers and legs and they responded. One side of my face seemed paralyzed, and it took a conscious effort to breathe, but I could see and hear clearly, and nothing seemed wrong with my mind—nothing that wasn't wrong to begin with. I tried to sit up.

"Easy," Doug said.

"What's it about, Eileen?" I asked. "Why did you sell us out to the Feddies? You did, didn't you?"

She was still crying. "Because you'll ruin everything," she said. "Your horrible Project. We're learning what causes ice ages on Earth, we're learning what makes planets, and you'll ruin all that! You can't, you just can't do it."

"Are there Feddie cops outside?" I asked.

"Yes. University police. My father sent them."

"And Dr. Weinbaum? Did you betray him, too?"

"I don't know—"

"You know Kehiayan's orders," Doug said. "They didn't get the Doc alive. . ."

"Worry about us. We've got to stay alive a little over twenty-five hours and blow that thing off," Plemmons said. "Got any suggestions, Lieutenant? I guess you're in charge again." His voice was heavy with sarcasm. I had that coming.

"I think I can get up," I said, and did it. "Okay. We've got to get help. The only help I know of is the drillers. If they haven't been arrested. And the only way we can find that out is to get out of here. How many air bottles have we got?"

"Enough."

"Get packs together and fill the water tanks in the suits. We need twenty-five hours worth of air and water. We'll skip food. Then we've got to figure a way out of here."

"I got a way," Plemmons said. "Blow out a wall with shaped charges. Stands to reason they're watchin' the air lock, not the back of the blockhouse. Blow it and run like hell."

"Will a blowout hurt the detonator?" I asked Erica.

"No. Are you really all right?"

"I'm going to live. I—"

"We'll talk about it later," she said.

"Yeah. Just what happened? How did you—I mean, why didn't she get the rest of you, too?"

Erica's eyes narrowed. "Because Don told me you'd been seeing her," she said. "And I heard her voice out here, and I watched her. And don't say I was spying on you, because I've got a right to know what my fiancé is doing! I'm not giving you up to some school-educated snob! So when she sprayed you with that stuff and closed up her faceplate, I came up behind her and knocked the can out of her hand and batted her head against the wall."

"I'm amazed you didn't kill her," I said. I said it to myself, but I must have been talking louder than I thought.

"I would have, but I thought we ought to find out what she'd done to you."

Lord save us, I thought. "Don, set the charges in the back wall of your room."

Plemmons nodded and went back into the blockhouse. "What do we do with the bitch?" Doug asked.

"Put her helmet on her, tie her up, and leave her," I said.

"Maybe I should spray inside the helmet with some of that gunk," Doug said. "Erica?"

Eileen's face went white. "You can't! You aren't—you can't?"

"No," Erica said. "But I'd like to. Wait a minute. What did you put in Garrett's coffee?"

Eileen didn't answer.

"Would it have killed him?" Erica demanded.

"No! It's just a knockout drop—"

"Drink it," Erica said. She brought the cup over. "Now, and every drop, or I swear I will use that spray can on you."

"But—"

Erica got the spray can.

"All right!" Eileen drank the coffee. They put her helmet on her and closed the faceplate. She sat still for a minute, then her head slowly nodded over.

"She could be faking," Erica said. "Tie her up, Doug."

"Right."

I got up and moved gingerly around the room. I could walk all right. My face still felt funny, the way it does after a jawful of novocaine, but otherwise I seemed okay. A little light-headed, maybe, but that could have been from the shots as much as anything. "I'll function," I said. "Okay, let's get ready."

We got our packs and weapons. Erica carried her detonator. "All set?" Plemmons asked.

"Yeah," I said. "Let her fly."

We heard the explosions, then whistling air, and then silence. Half the wall was blown out. We leaped through, and Doug and Erica ran off toward the derrick. Plemmons and I ran to either side and wheeled around.

Someone fired at us from the dark. There were the silent orange flowers I remembered from the Deucalion battle. A figure moved toward me, and I swung the submachine gun like a hose, cutting him down. I fired another burst, then ran off after Erica.

Plemmons dropped down behind some rocks. "Move, chief," he said. His voice was loud in my headset.

"No heroes," I ordered. "Need all of us—"

"Be along in a minute." He fired a burst with his automatic rifle, and I ran on, wondering if I'd ever see him again.

We'd let the drillers guard the wellhead because, short of drilling out the hole again, there was no way the bomb could be disturbed. They'd been taking the rig apart and stowing it for travel, so we weren't too worried that anybody would drill for the bomb.

It was a kilometer to the well site. About halfway I felt woozy. This looked like as good a place to make a stand as any. I found a boulder and got behind it.

A figure came running toward me out of the dark. I sighted on it. "Don?" I called into the mike.

"Yeah, chief, don't get nervous."

"Leapfrog," I said. "Move on."

He slowed and looked around but couldn't see where I was.

"Go." I ordered.

He ran past, and I waited. My eyes were getting accustomed to starlight, and Deimos, the outer moon, was up. Deimos doesn't give much light; it's not even a disk, just a very bright star, but it was something. I thought I saw movement in front of me and fired a burst.

More orange flowers answered me. At least a dozen. I tried to remember where they'd been, and fired at a couple I was sure of. More answering fire from out there.

I didn't think I'd hit anybody. We stayed that way, trading silent shots for several minutes, and then I decided it was time to get the hell out of there. I crawled into a deep shadow and began to move toward the drill site.

Something bumped against me. I grabbed it, and we rolled over in the dark, tearing at each other. My weapon was tugged out of my hands. I reached back onto my belt and got my knife and thrust it, then again. Again. I felt him go limp, and hoped I hadn't run into one of my friends. Then I felt around for my submachine gun and crawled farther into the shadow. Finally I got up and ran.

"Garrett!" It was Erica's voice. I wished for air, so I could tell where she was.

"Coming!" I called.

"Hurry. We've got a tractor—"

"They're listening," I reminded her.

"I know that. Hurry."

"Sure. Count off!"

"Plemmons."

"Barston."

So Doug and Don had both made it. And Erica. I was breathing hard as I got to the well site. There wasn't anyone around that I could see.

"To your left," Erica's voice said.

I ran off into the darkness and almost fell over them. There were four drillers as well. "This way," a voice said. One of the drillers moved off, and we followed. He went around a boulder the size of a palace, and there was a tractor behind it.

"Get on," the driller said. We climbed on top of it, and it began moving off, upward, up the side of the volcano. It made sense; the cops were down below, and we couldn't go that way, but I didn't much like the idea of climbing that hill. Suppose we were still there when it was time to set off the bomb?

I moved toward Erica. There was something bothering

me. It had for a couple of days, but I hadn't needed to know before. Now I did. I took her shoulder and moved my helmet next to hers. "Radio off," I said.

"Off. What do you think you're doing? Let me go."

"Damn it, save being mad for later—"

"I will. Believe me."

"I believe you. I have to know something. That bomb's a couple of kilometers underground. There's no radio signal can go through that kind of rock. There must be a wire connection, something like that."

"Something like that," she said.

"What? Can they get at it and disable it?"

"It's a transponder. A receiver picks up the detonator signal and sends a sonic pulse through the ground," Erica said. "It's well hidden."

"Does Drury know about this?" I asked.

"Did you? He's a scientist, so he knows there has to be one—but he has no more idea *where* than you do."

"All right. But you had to have help. Who does know?"

"Tex. The Skipper said we could trust him. And he's driving the tractor."

"Okay." Now I had time to pay attention to what was happening to us. We were driving, without lights, at maybe twenty kilometers an hour, which doesn't sound very fast until you think about it. The road was narrow and getting narrower, and we were headed up the side of the mountain. I didn't think we were likely to be coming back down.

I pulled Erica closer to me. "Sweetheart, I'm sorry—"

"I don't want to talk about it."

"All right."

"You damned fool!"

She did want to talk about it. She had a lot to say while we went up that mountain, up a goddamn mountain that we were going to turn into a volcano in about twenty-four hours.

Boy did she want to talk about it.

18

We stopped about two kilometers from the drill site. When dawn came we'd dug in. Nobody had bothered us. There wasn't but one way up, and we had that covered, with the tractor's lights shining down on the road below.

"We in range for your gadget?" I asked Erica.

"Yes."

"Then there's nothing for it but to wait," I said. "Doug, have you got anything we can raise the Skipper with?"

"No. Not with us."

"That worries me," I said. "They'll try to get to him and tell him it's all off. Or something—"

"Won't matter a lot," Plemmons said. "Plan's movin' now. Agents have gone up front. Skipper won't call it off, too much at stake now. Not unless you tell him yourself."

"Maybe. I'd sure like to get through to him," I said.

I looked around at my tiny command. Tex and Cal and two other drillers. Don and Doug. And Erica. Eight of us. I wondered how many Feddies were down below.

"I'll have a go," Doug said.

"No," I told him.

"My job, Garrett. I'm communications. And you're needed up here—"

"I'm not needed at all."

"You got a job to do," Doug said. "It won't end when that bomb goes unless—" he turned toward Erica. "Anyway, it's your job, not mine. Mine's communications, and I know where the sets are. Maybe I can sneak through. These aren't Marsmen, you know. University cops. Townmen. No good out in the open. I'll be safer than you are."

"All right," I said. "How will you go?"

"Around west and down the draw. Cross the road when I think I can. Hell, it's a piece of cake." Doug waved and was gone.

We waited. Nothing happened. The sun got higher.

"Did Eileen know when H-hour was?" Erica asked.

"Not from me. Did Drury?"

"Of course. But I don't think he would tell them—"

"He will if they ask right. The way you asked Eileen what she'd done to me. Did you mean any of that?"

"I don't have to say."

"*I* believed you," I said.

"I wish they'd do something," Erica said.

"Maybe they think they can wait us out. Have you heard any chatter on the radios?" She had been tuning back and forth across the different bands.

"No. But they could be using very low power."

"Probably are."

We waited some more. The sun got higher, and it warmed up a bit. It was going to be damned cold out there for the night, with only the tractor as a place to warm up.

"I'm getting hungry," I said. "I could—"

"Hush. Listen." She showed me the frequency. I tuned to it.

"Pittson? Can you hear us?"

I thought about whether we should answer. Why not? "Yeah, I hear you. Who is that?"

"Captain Moncrief, Federation police. Your rebellion has been called off, Pittson. Your Commander Farr has been broadcasting that the big push is not on after all. You may as well give up."

"Bullshit."

"It's true."

"I don't care if it is. I've got my orders."

167

"What do you think is going to happen to you when you detonate that weapon?" Moncrief asked.

"I try not to think about it. But I'm gonna do it. Guess when?"

"I know when."

"Good for you."

"Pittson, give us the detonator and we'll send you home. Back to Hellas. You and all your people. We don't want you. But what you're doing is insane."

Trouble was, he was probably right.

"I'm getting something else," Erica said. "Here."

I changed bands. There was nothing but static, then: "Blowhole, this is Highguard. We know your status. Your orders are unchanged. Garrett, if you're listening, we have the message. Hope you can hear this." The message repeated several times.

"The ship," I said. "Doug must have got through. Hope he's all right."

We waited some more.

They rushed us just before dark. It was stupid. They had no chance of knocking us off before we could set off the bomb. They could make us trigger it twelve hours early, but they couldn't stop us.

They didn't even manage that. We cut down five of them as they came up the road, and I think I got another in the rocks off to our left. It wasn't much of a battle. They didn't have any better weapons than we did.

An hour later they tried something else. First they called and got me to talk, then they let us hear a man groaning.

"That's your communications man," Moncrief said. "We don't like hurting people, Pittson. But there's too much at stake here. Give up, and we'll let him go. And you, too. All of you. We'll send you home."

"Bugger yourself."

There were more groans and a couple of screams.

"I think that is Doug," Plemmons said. "Bastards. Dirty bastards."

"Can't take that," Cal said. He moved off before anyone could stop him. A few minutes later we saw gunfire below.

"Cal," Tex called. "Answer me, you black bastard!"

"Got a couple, gettin' more." His voice sounded pinched.

"He's losing pressure," Tex said. "Oh Goddamn."

There were more shots and a grenade went off below. Again no sound, only the flashes. Then nothing.

A sniper hit Plemmons about midnight. We got him into the tractor so he wouldn't freeze and left him to care for himself if he could. He'd been hit on the right side, just below the rib cage. It didn't look good.

"Pittson's Last Stand," I told Erica. "Come on." I led her away from the tractor, a little higher up the mountain and off to one side. We kept the radios off. I had a sleeping bag from out of the tractor, and we managed to get that around us. There was a wind whipping past, but it was very thin, not any real problem.

We huddled together, helmets touching. "I've been thinking," Erica said. "I want a wood table. Why should mother have the only wood table on the Rim? Will you make me a wood table, Gary?"

"Have to wait for the tree to grow," I said.

"Sure. No problem. They say people on Mars can live to be two hundred. We've got plenty of time."

"I love you."

"I hope so. I wish we weren't all sealed up in these suits and stuff. I wonder how Eskimos manage to be affectionate? There are Eskimos on Mars. Did you know that?"

"Sure. I met the Greatstars at a Rim gatherin'. Be good to see them again. Wonder how the Skipper's making out with his speech? Wish we could hear it."

"Garrett, what time is it?"

"Five minutes later than the last time you asked."

"O God. I was sure I'd waited three hours."

There were flashes out to the left, where the tractor was. They were firing again. The fools. It went on for a long time.

There were twinges of light in the east. "Two minutes to go," I told her. "You ready? Box didn't freeze?"

"No. I designed it to take this. Or almost anything else."

"I damn near froze my balls off—"

"I hope not," she said.

"Yeah. I haven't heard anything on the radio for hours—"

"No. Is it time?"

"Coming up. I love you. Five. I always did. Four. Three. Two. One. Go"

She pressed the keys. Almost immediately we felt a sharp whump! and the ground shook beneath us. Then we felt rumbling. When we pressed our helmets against the rocks we could hear it, a long rumbling sound like thunder that wouldn't go away.

The rim of the sun came over the horizon. The plain below us was still dark, but there was light shining on us and on the mountain peak. The sky above us was still dead black velvet with stars against it.

The rumble went on, then the stars began to fade, and there was a peculiar color to the sky above. White clouds shot upward toward the stars, white cloud with red tinges, then solid chunks of red.

"It worked!" Erica screamed. "Garrett, it worked! The Project! It worked!"

"Yeah." It sure had. Streaks of fire shot upward and the entire mountain shook. The white vapor climbed higher and higher into the sky, then condensed. Snowflakes and hail began to fall around us, mixed with redhot rock that flew out of the rim in a much lower arc.

Fire and ice. I stood and threw back my head and roared laughter and defiance and every other emotion. "Fire and ice. A new world born in fire and ice!" I was fascinated with the image. It was the first poetic thought I'd ever had. I liked it. I said it again, "A new world born in fire and ice."

Sanity came back almost too late. "We've got to get the hell out of here—"

"The Feddies—" Erica shouted.

"Bugger the Feddies. They're running too. Let's go!"

We dashed down the mountain toward the tractor. When we got closer we saw bodies around it. Tex, his faceplate smashed open. Another driller. The door of the tractor stood open, and there was a body there, too. A Feddie cop with a knife in his chest.

Don Plemmons lay inside the tractor. He was stiff as a board, and there was a huge icicle of blood on his chest. His hand was still curled, as if he were gripping the knife he'd thrust into the Federation policeman.

170

"There's nobody alive here," I shouted. "Help me get Plemmons out—"

"We can't leave him! He should be buried—"

"He will be!" I pointed up the mountain. A red glow was pouring over the edge. "He will be! It's his monument, his and Tex's and—" I tried to remember the driller's name, but I couldn't. "Come on."

We dragged the stiffened corpse out of the tractor. I had time to lay Don so that his enemy was at his feet. Then I prayed, silently; the tractor started.

There was enough sunlight to move it. I got the wings extended and there was more power. We drove down the road. A chunk of rock hit the deck of the tractor, destroying some of the solar cells. It slowed but went on. We rolled over boulders that had fallen in the road or pushed them aside. Once we went off the road and up onto the side of the hill to get around a big one.

Then we were in the flat below. Fire and ice still fell around us, but not so thick now. We drove on, across the plateau to the road down to the next level. When we turned off, we faced three tractors.

We had no armament except my submachine gun.

"They've got us," Erica said. "I—you're not—they can't take me. I—"

"Crap. By now the revolution worked or it didn't. I don't care if they know how many bombs we have, or how we make them, or—"

"But—"

"But nothing!" I picked up my weapon and worked the bolt. "Well, General Pittson strikes again. Pittson, hero of Pittson's Last Stand, Pittson's Disaster, Pittson's Retreat, Pitt—"

"Shut up and listen!" she said. "Look, those aren't Feddie tractors!"

The tractors had stopped. A man got out of the lead vehicle and stood with his arms waving at us.

"It's Doug," I said. "He must have gone to our station contacts for help." I tuned through the frequency band until I heard him.

"We did it," Doug was shouting. "We did it! They're rioting in every city! Mars General Company has declared for Free Mars! We've won! Garrett, Erica, we've won! Goddamn it, we've won."

Epilogue

We were married a month later. Sarge stood up for me. He had some new medals for his uniform. When Commander Farr offered to fight the man who said I wasn't a Marsman I couldn't help crying.

Best of all, the Padre told Erica never to mention Eileen again. But she didn't give her word. . .

47